# Gold and Myrrh

# Gold and Myrrh

*Paul Keller*

## K A Nitz
ALBANY, NEW ZEALAND

*Gold und Myrrhe* first published
in German 1898

This translation into New Zealand English
Copyright © K A Nitz 2019
All rights reserved

ISBN: 978-0-473-49833-7

# Contents

Introduction: Gold and Myrrh.......................7

Franz Seyfried.....................................9

Little Rose by the Way....................21

Wilted Leaf.....................................35

A Springtime Folktale....................41

Poor Children...................................55

Fate (Two Short Tales)....................69

The Old and the New School Cupboard.......81

The Tramp.........................................93

Mountain Peace...........................107

Forge Fire (A Character Study)...................137

# INTRODUCTION:
# GOLD AND MYRRH

"They presented unto him gifts; gold, and frankincense, and myrrh."* Frankincense because he was God, but gold and myrrh because he was a man.

The people — gold and myrrh! A clever idea! Was it thought up, by those who are called "wise men", on the long journey to Judea, or was it obvious?

Oh, in the tents of the East, they knew quite surely bleak and cheerful, good and bad, shimmering fortune and bitter hardship, they knew human fate. Thus the thoughtful mind easily found a symbol — the human gift of gold and myrrh.

For Christ, the gift had an especially apt significance, because he was not only a man, but also a teacher of men. And so really gold and myrrh also always lay close next to one another in his life. Here the flaming gold of his shining love, there the myrrh of indifference; here a shimmering seed of thankfully returned love, there the bitter herbs of misjudgement, and ever and ever success and failure, and ever and ever gold and myrrh. —

And his great, tragic lot became all the little ones who are named after the teacher in their masses. Even over their creating, striving and struggling, there often lies a red, shimmering light, bright as gold; but also

---

* Matthew 2:11.

7

growing rampantly in their lives — and not the least in their own hearts — are many a little plant, bitter as myrrh.

I have also called you, little book, "Gold and Myrrh", because you shall tell of the teacher's life, and because hence the message of joy and the news of sorrow must stand close next to one another in you. — You step out on a long journey, the journey into the land of men. And before you go, I want to say to you, 'You will share in the fate of those of whom you narrate, what you will also find out there in the land of men is gold and myrrh!'

# FRANZ SEYFRIED

N., 5<sup>th</sup> May 1885.

Little Franz Seyfried is decidedly an original; I want to make notes about him in my diary.

An original, — dear God! In the truthfully written histories of human society, an original is deemed surely to be a significant or interesting personality, the backward philistinism calls its strong individuals "funny oddballs", and the poor folk call everything which deviates from the line of the everyday simply "crazy".

And Franz Seyfried is poor!

His grandmother is the widow of a count's forester who was shot by poachers in the exercise of his duty. The Count gifted the old woman a cottage at the end of the village and tossed her a small annuity. On that she lives.

She had an only daughter; this girl went into the wide world as the wife of an actor. Years later, she returned to die at home. She left behind for the old woman, other than some colourful junk, little Franz. He has now been my student for five weeks.

He is not especially tall for his age, yet a fine-limbed figure. His eyes are deep, veiled, mysterious, his locks full and wild. He has conspicuously small hands and remarkably long ears. That should be a barely deceptive sign of intellectual ability. Actually he is not good-looking; it also does no harm, or rather does good as he would otherwise have long since not been so interesting.

He is a fabulously bad student, surely because he is by far the most gifted of all. Whatever interests the other children of his age is incidental and boring to him. During lessons, he mostly gazes apathetically at the ceiling. I have until now had no influence at all over him. He has no confidence in me, I think he hates me. I must of course prefer having him all the more.

Just the once, I have seen his dark fervent eyes light up; they are in such a moment quite indescribably beautiful. I announced to him I wanted to tell a folk tale now. But hardly had I begun than he was again apathetic, and when I asked him at the end whether he liked the folk tale, he said, "No, I knew it already, and my grandmother also tells it much better."

His grandmother — that I believe; she is also such a sort of original. She must tell the boy many stories, particularly about his beautiful, unfortunate mother, and all she experienced and acted out in the wide world.

She has a significant influence on the boy, but even without her, he would be what he is.

4$^{th}$ June.

I have now quite often met little Seyfried outside, most often before the windmill. There he lies in the middle of the windmiller's lawn, and listens for hours to the clattering of the mill. —

Today I had to punish a bigger boy because of stubborn lies. Little Franz was present at the time. That was very incautious of me. He had by then already become somewhat more trusting, but now of course the arduously obtained progress was again forfeited.

After the lesson, I felt something tugging on my coat. It was Franz with his little, white hand. He gazed up at me. What a look! A mixture of fear and anger, pleading and threatening.

"Hey," he said, "I will never lie to you; but you must not strike me either!"

27<sup>th</sup> June.

I discover almost daily something strange in Franz Seyfried. His presence is so strong that it frequently expresses itself.

Today a bigger boy knocked over a little girl on the school path right before the schoolhouse. The poor thing dirtied her hands badly and her face too, and began crying bitterly. The malefactor toddled off as quickly as possible of course. Franz was just then also coming along the path. When he saw the hardship of the child, he paused, seized her energetically by the hand, and drew her to the well. There he washed the girl's face and hands thoroughly, and dried everything off well with the sleeves of his bright shirt. Little Eva acquiesced to it gladly, and then stood with fresh-washed, little red face laughing before him. Franz gazed for a while, and then — I thought I was dreaming — he embraced her around the neck with a cry of jubilation and — kissed her. — — Right on the lips!

3<sup>rd</sup> July.

If it did not sound so venal, I would maintain in all seriousness that my little, seven year old student Franz Seyfried is — with the same aged, little Eva Werner — smitten.

Every morning he waits for half an hour and more before her house to be able to cover the path to school just with her. In the afternoons, she herds the geese; at the same time, he keeps her company. I have observed them both recently.

They were sitting with one another on the side of the path. She was chattering very cheerfully, he was silent.

But he was constantly looking her in the face. Then she made him a wreath of cornflowers and field poppies. Then he kissed her again.

It was bad weather on Tuesday, and the geese excursion had to remain undone. Franz thus could not come together with Eva. There he shall have cried again for the first time in a long time. For he does not go to her parents. He never goes to other people. His grandmother does not want him to either; she has become almost unsociable as a result of the tragic fates of her husband and her daughter.

So odd, this affair with Franz! Goethe was meant to have loved for the first time at nine years old, why should Seyfried not at seven! — — But it is too hilarious, it cannot be! One thing is definite though, it is not a mere childhood friendship, at least not with Franz. What is it then? And what should I do? My old pedagogy leaves me entirely in the lurch here; it does that also with significantly simpler cases. I believe the best thing which I can do is to do nothing.

6th August.

Today I have made a sad discovery with Franz — he is inclined towards vindictiveness.

It was a hot day. In the school premises we unfortunately have a vexatious number of flies a lot of the time. It is just now thus in the countryside.

A fly lands on the forehead of little Seyfried. He reluctantly grimaces. That helps momentarily, but the fly returns. That happens thus twice, three times. At the same time, a dark redness climbs in the boy's face. Now the fly is sitting on his left hand. His dark eyes assume now a cat-like, lurking expression. Now his face twitches, the fly has bitten him. At the same moment, however, he has caught it.

He observes the captured creature for a while. His face has become quite red, a light, moaning sound comes from his lips. I call his name admonishingly; he does not hear, and in the next moment tears both wings of the fly. He lets it run, and at the same time his eyes gleam like those of a panther.

I hurry now to his place, kill the martyred creature first, and reproach his deed then in severe words as something loathsome. To that he simply says, "It tormented me, and I tormented it too."

Then my patience cracks, I turn away with a vigorous movement to the cupboard in which my cane lies locked. On the way, I fortunately look around once.

There he sits with staring eyes, deathly pale face and trembling limbs. He must not be beaten — never; with him the blow would not strike the hand, but rather the heart.

But his defiance! Then a thought comes to me.

"Eva, come here! You see, a fly, which does not know any better, annoyed Franz. Then he caught it and tore both its wings from its body. Tell him what that is!"

Eva stands with tear-filled eyes before him, she does not look at him; quietly, but firmly, she then says, "That is bad!"

A gurgling sound comes from the boy's lips, he grasps for his heart with a hand, and as if struck by lightning, he sinks under the bench.

I could not soothe him anymore. I believe certainly that he is becoming ill.

That was a difficult day!

In September.

I have never believed in the theory of inheritance of traits; now I would like to allow an exception. Little Seyfried has acting blood like his parents.

He is reconciled with Eva, he also does not seem to hold a grudge against me anymore. But every time a fly lands on his face, he trembles gently. But he leaves the creature unharmed.

Recently I saw him while walking through the fields together with a crowd of children. They were sitting or crouching in regular rows one behind the other. As I looked closer, I saw little Seyfried standing before them, gesticulating animatedly.

I stepped closer. The children were not disturbed when I stepped into their circle of play; they are used to it. I stepped quietly behind the last row, and then what the children were playing became clear to me — theatre. Just then Franz announced, "The new play about Sleeping Beauty."

He narrated almost everything, but in an unusually animated way. At places of verbal speech, he assumed the appropriate pose, and he performed individual acts. Everything used hand and foot, and the means of expression was directly astounding for a seven year old boy.

Towards the end of the play, Eva received the familiar kiss and the school bully the historic slap in the face. The latter called forth such a storm of applause that the show had to end.

But I went home, deep in thought.

6th May (two years later).

There are theatre people in the village tavern, proper theatre people, not a puppet show.

Franz is completely rapt. Almost the entire day, he stands before the village tavern, and when the show is meant to begin, it is as if he is seized by a fever. He has to get in! Fortunately, apart from Birch-Pfeiffer melodramas, mostly only 'classic' plays are performed.

"Fortunately", I mean that of course only in reference to Franz, for otherwise — dear misery!

The grandmother has no objections to Franz's rage for the theatre, but she of course cannot buy a ticket every day. But he must get in, that is definite!

All of a sudden, he is taken in amongst the ninepin boys. Previously he rejected such a suggestion proudly.

Now he shall have thereby committed quite a dishonest act. It is custom hereabouts that the ninepin man, whenever all nine pins fall at the same time, pays the ninepin boys a special reward of one pfennig. That certainly does not happen too frequently at all. Usually the one pin to the left remains standing, and even with a good bowler only eight fall.

There Franz now shall have placed a string under the ninth, stubbornly remaining pin and from time to time have perfected the player's luck.

I did not trust him, and asked him. Then he said, "I invented it, but I don't like doing it."

And he did not lie. Since that time, however, he has not liked setting up pins anymore.

Since he now has absolutely no money to be able to go to the theatre, he hires himself out to the troop for all sorts of services. He cleans shoes, washes, hauls water and wood, plays the errand boy; he who is usually such a proud boy. As avidly as it may draw him to the theatre, what of everything might assail him during these days! Should I forbid him from visiting the theatre?

14th May.

The shock stabs me all over even now. I am sitting in the arbour, right by the garden fence. Then I hear his voice. Hastily, in whispering tones, I hear him say, "I want to tell you, Eva, but you promise me that you won't reveal it."

"Eh, where would I then, Franz!"

"You see, Eva, tomorrow the theatre is moving on, and — and — you see — my father, my mother — Eva, it just won't work any other way, won't work, won't work — I must go with them!"

I hear the girl immediately shriek out, then I am through the hedge with a few powerful movements.

Franz stands before me as if turned to stone; I seize him by the hand.

"Come with me to your grandmother!"

He cries out.

"Oh God — no, no — she'll die, she'll die!"

"She — will die? And do you think she won't die if you run away from her into the wide world! Has she earned this thanks from you, your good grandmother?"

Then he sinks to his knees before me, and seizes my hand. Hot, like glowing metal, his tears fall on it.

"I suffered so — I did not think it through properly! I certainly don't want to go away, only promise me you won't tell her — just — just because else she will die."

15th May.

This excitement! I had intended to keep a sharp eye on Franz, but he vanished almost without a sound.

My shock is great. I hurry to the old Seyfried. I do not reveal the truth to her, but ask merely incidentally after Franz. She knows nothing of him, and is afraid.

Now I run to the "director" of the theatre. I take him sharply to task. He becomes brusque, and does not want to know anything.

I am besides myself. Three, four times, I run about the village, I ask everywhere — in vain! I even run into the forest, I shout his name on all the paths — in vain! He is not by the windmill either. An indescribable fear befalls me. By the millpond, where I stop, a terrible thought comes to me. "Merciful God, just not that!"

Now, back home again! "Now I will reveal everything to fetch help", I decide. There — in the yard, right by my woodpile, I hear his voice, "Teacher!"

"Franz! You're alive! Praise God! Where are you hiding then?"

"Here in the woodshed, the key must lie a bit before the door!"

So it is. I quickly unlock it. Franz stands before me.

"For all the world, what are you up to here?"

He asks humbly and quietly, "Are they gone?"

"Who?"

"Well, the actors!"

"Yes, yes, but what does this mean?"

"I, I had promised you that I wouldn't go away with them, and then my grandmother — but, it was just so difficult; if I had seen the wagons going — perhaps I would then have forgotten everything — and — and — then I fetched the key here from the kitchen, and locked myself in from within, and out the vent —"

"Went the key!", I rejoiced, and kissed the courageous boy — smack on the lips.

16th May.

I spoke with the Pastor. He wants to give Franz foreign language lessons, and if the Count takes it further then, if God wills it, a genuine artist will be made of Franz someday.

I cannot describe how happy I am. My dear, courageous, divinely gifted, glorious Franz! It cannot fail, he will become a great man. A great man, I am quite silly! Franz, ah — ah!

When I told him about the Pastor, he cried, and I with him. —

In June (four years later).

Franz is now going on fourteen. He has become tall and very handsome. When a stranger goes through the village and sees him by chance, he certainly pauses. For you do not see such a face often, and can never forget it either.

And he is good! I know of no single material fault in him. He has hot blood surely, but he knows how to control it wonderfully. Whenever the red of fury climbs in his face, he bites his teeth together and shakes his head energetically. Then he is calm.

Despite his excellent qualities, he has much to suffer in the village. How could it be otherwise? He is an original, and the people understand only everyday sights. And if man different from what they see everyday comes before their eyes, it annoys them, and they themselves get angry. It can be no other way.

Intellectually, Franz has made great progress; he has almost proceeded with seven league boots. The Pastor says he could pass with honour in one of the highest classes of the elite high school. I am pleased no end! Franz is simply my quite special hope, my quite special love.

He does not kiss Eva anymore; but I know that he carries in his breast pocket a small picture which she gifted him. May he carry it, and may it be a talisman on his heart and in his heart — one day! One day, when he has struggled up through his genius and his effort — ah, to where?!

Mid-June.

There was now always a great air of secrecy amongst the children; Franz seemed also to have something to do with the matter. Today I gave learnt everything. A quite little boy comes to me and says, "Teacher, we are giving a play on your birthday, which Seyfried taught us. But you must not say anything!"

That I have not done either, and so good Franz has also not learnt that his secret has been betrayed.

# Franz Seyfried

10<sup>th</sup> September.

Whether I am really writing it down? It is certainly madness, madness three times over, ghosts of hell, what I know — it is not true, cannot be true, what the people say, no, no, no! Franz Seyfried, they say, is a murderer. Is that not, not — laughable? But — but — they all say it, and I, I also saw it myself. Saw it myself! Merciful God!

I must collect myself, I must write it down at once though, I think otherwise I will end up in a fluster.

It was on the 6<sup>th</sup> July, on my birthday. In the morning, Franz brought me a bouquet and a poem he had composed. At the same time, he told me that he had written a little festive play and rehearsed it with the schoolchildren. I was deeply moved.

In the afternoon, the festive play was to be performed in the schoolroom. In the place of the teacher's desk, a stage was erected by the wall, a pair of boards over two trestles.

Before the performance, after everything lay ready, Franz had locked the door. I shall have been the first to enter the space.

We walked over together, the Pastor and I; also many people from the village were in attendance. When Franz now opened the door, he saw just then how the school bully was climbing out the window. The school bully had always been a rough, devious rascal. Franz disclosed to me that he had to exclude the bully from the play because of his incompatibility, then he drew back to dress himself up a little.

Now the show was meant to begin. Then — — — I cannot go on today, I will continue writing tomorrow.

11<sup>th</sup> September.

Franz wants to enter the podium as the first, then — a crash, and he falls down. The school bully has sawn the boards. A shock flies through the assembly, a silence occurs, only the bully laughs, loud, raw, ungovernably.

Then — like a raging lion, Franz springs forth, in a second he is around the neck of the bully, a gurgling, a fall; Franz and the bully are lying on the floor. — In the bully's chest, a knife is stuck — in the middle of his heart. —

Out of my mind, I stand with the Pastor next to the body and next to Franz. He lies impotently on the floor with stiff limbs; white foam is before his mouth.

For days I have actually been without a clear mind. I struggled like a madman with the police, who wanted to lead Franz away. —

His old grandmother has gone mad; she will soon have overcome it.

My glorious, my only Franz, my hope, my love!

And that is the end! — — —

15th October.

Today the court has adjudged that Franz Seyfried is to be committed to prison for four years.

Four years!!

How will he come back?

Broken, corrupted, lost!

God, have you no light in this terrible night?!

All Souls' Day (2nd November).

God is good. Eight days ago, Franz Seyfried died. The Pastor himself gave him the last rites. I will never forget it, the last look of those beautiful eyes.

My poor, poor friend! Rest in peace! I will pray for you, today on All Soul's Day and always, always!

# LITTLE ROSE BY THE WAY

The dusk! A peculiar magic lies in the word and above all in the time itself.

In the ghostly twilight, in the vague half-darkness, the impossible appears possible, happiness eternal, but also the shadow of misfortune gigantic; and just like the dreamer at dusk weaves his dreams and ideals from thousands of colourful threads into a cloth, the fortunate man's happiness will burst from his chest at dusk, and the unfortunate man is never so scared before his misfortune as in the shadow of the falling night.

At dusk memory likes most of all to rise from the grave and step up to people, and mix in their hearts old joys and old sorrows into gentle wistfulness. And the sheltering darkness hides its quiet workings so that no idle eye intercepts it.

It was at dusk. I sat with my friend, on that day like I often did. My friend is a very proficient musician, a famous man. I may say that, although I am his friend.

His study has a very simple furnishing, though a comfortable armchair is by the window. I hog it mostly. You have there by the window a very beautiful view onto a magnificent, peaceful garden. In this garden there are very tall, old trees and — no people.

My friend is playing on his violin. He mostly does that at dusk. At the same time, he walks up and down the room, and he sometimes pauses leaning against the wall. Today he has at my request played "The Legend" by a famous master, and in addition a few variations on an old nursery rhyme. He is playing that for himself, and there it is always more beautiful than when I desire something for myself.

When you listen to good music from time to time, you learn first to divine its sense, then to feel it, then to comprehend it; feeling remains, however, always the principal thing. Thus I listen also today more with my heart than with my mind.

To start with, it is not difficult to comprehend the music. The violin pours forth a charming tale, a tale or a picture, and the content is the scent of flowers, birdsong, the murmuring of springs, the rustling of the forest — May. But then the birdsong passes over into a human song. For no bird sings thus, not even the nightingale; only people have such notes, when they exult and lament, and quiver and hope and fear in their songs of love.

Then the sweet air breaks off abruptly, a deep note disturbs the lovely harmony.

Is it meant thus? There the idea lies clearly — May, the happiness of love, separation — the old song. The motif would, however, be too stale for the good musician, there must be something else behind it.

The deeper note returns again, but it does not sound as lamenting or as shrill as it would sound when it describes common circumstances. A mute agony lies in this note, a fearful question, a defiant rebelling, a hoping and doubting. From time to time, the melody flies up again into a passionate passage for the love motif. In vain, it falls back! And then the air breaks off. It finishes with a lofty note, not shrilly as I expected. That was a farewell, anguished but voluntary, unhappy but without ill will.

# Little Rose by the Way

My friend stands remotely by the wall. Despite the darkness, I believe I detect how he is trembling. And then what I heard becomes clear to me — it's a musical confession.

A pause — then the violin starts up again, this time with an adagio from Beethoven. I understand my friend, he wants to soothe himself.

But what I heard does not leave my mind. I brood, brood, and do not come to a clear understanding. And yet I believe I feel the right thing.

A pencil lies on the windowsill, and a piece of paper. Entirely in darkness, I begin writing — a few verses as they come to mind just then.

> I saw along my way
> A rose is standing,
> It laughs at me
> Young and pretty.
> It mustn't look for long
> Melting and crimson,
> I have to move on,
> Little rose, God protect you!

The adagio has ended. My friend makes a few more strides through the room, then he lights a lamp. I quickly want to hide my jottings; but he has already caught sight of me.

"You are writing?"

"A few verses without rhymes, nothing clever — let them be!"

He gazes with a peculiarly inquiring look at me.

"Show!"

"As I said, there is nothing to them — no rhymes — reminiscences. —"

"Please, don't be childish and vain," he says nervously, and tears the page from my hand.

With reading through it, his pale face turns red. He holds his head lowered for a little while, then he looks up abruptly with his large eyes.

"You understood — *that*?"

And he pointed with his head to the violin.

"Understood? — No! Only felt in the outlines."

He reads the verses once more.

"It matches, matches it exactly even! I certainly believe that it is not really clear to you what you are writing. But you have felt it properly — instinctively. It lies in it, quite certainly! It lies in the words 'It mustn't look for long', and in the 'I have to move on', in particular the 'I have to'."

"But it is just the reason for this 'have to' that I don't understand!"

"You desire an exposition?"

"I don't desire anything at all. You know that I did not want to surrender the verses to you, also I am not so indiscreet to ask you about previous experiences."

He obviously did not take it badly at all that I related the entire matter to him. He just silently nodded his head. Then he sat down by me.

"Leave the thing to me then, your rhymeless verses please me regardless, and it is suited to me. I want to compose myself a melody for it."

We sat for a little while in silence opposite each other. Then he began with a quiet, excited voice, "The memory has seized me violently, I want to tell it to you."

We remain at first with your image of the little rose. When you find one by the path, blossoming just then, fresh, charming, and it nods to you amiably with its little head, "Take me, take me!", then you just pluck it off, and anyone who doesn't is a fool. So at least do your everyday people think.

# Little Rose by the Way

I found such a little rose, young, beautiful, lovely, ah, what am I saying, I cannot describe it, you cannot comprehend it — you have not seen her. And the beautiful little rose did not say to me, "I will prick you!", but to start with, glowed still lovelier under my gaze, and then the eyes opened, and quietly, like a sweet breath, the "Yes" penetrated into my breast when I desired it. And the gardener who cherished it, to whom it was special, had not refused me it. But, when I desired it most of all, I moved on, and left it standing in its place, because I thought there it could live, and it would have to die on my breast if I carried it away. And that all happened as I will now relate.

I was a young fellow, cheerful, exuberant, light-headed, volatile, just like young fellows are. I was also gifted, as people assured me, and had that which most diverts young musicians, especially performers — money. Besides that, I stood entirely free then, and could do and not do whatever I liked.

I was in Italy for a long time. For almost a year, I stood under the impression of that wondrous and blissful land as though spellbound. By and by, I accustomed myself to the at first overpowering total impression, and began to make specialties of the delights. I lived alternately for the love of travel, the needs of performers, and the sheer delights. I achieved in every single thing that which was at all possible. Thus three years passed, then I became homesick.

It seemed to me as if my eyes hurt from the eternal golden reflections under the southern sky, as if my music, after I had formed so much around it, was no longer the pure heart's confidante it had once been, as if the beautiful woman that is Rome had poisoned my heart. I was ill and wanted to go home.

When I breathed the alpine air, I felt that I was very ill, but that I could recover at home. At home? Yes, where in all the world was my home? About this time, I cursed my isolated position in life, for which cheerful comrades had envied me often enough.

Then my only relative I still had occurred to me, the sister of my mother. She possessed a pretty country estate in Austria. I went to her and was taken in affectionately.

It was a charming, idyllic mountain village in which my aunt was the estate owner. Now, after many a long year, the most charming parties from it and its surrounds appear vividly before my eyes; the fantastic little rococo castle, the melancholy sawmiller by the brook, the little, deep blue pond which the people called "the lake", by its edge the melancholy meadows, the cheerful beech forest, the lovely little church on the hill, and the schoolhouse with its blossoming little garden — ah, the schoolhouse.

A sweet peace overcame me, the benevolent feeling of having saved myself from the bustle of the great world with its passions and wearying enticements at just the right hour into a quiet refuge where I could think for myself again, and find myself again. I was happy without a wish, and when my aunt asked me whether a loose rambling man like me would one day be oppressed by boredom in such a constricted resting place, I kissed her hand laughing.

On Sundays, I went to church with my aunt. The first time I was there, however, was in the evening. It was May's devotion. The communion sang a simple hymn, soberly accompanied by the deeply resounding organ. On the altar, only a few candles burned, the entirety made a right modest impression. But I was wondrously captivated. This mystical semidarkness, this deep, still peace, this heart-refreshing devotion of pious mountain residents made such a deep impression on me that a yearning arose in me to also be as pious and as pure as these people and share in the peace of their hearts. And at the end a hymn to Mary, a mixture of devotion, melancholy, and aching for heaven, a genuine hymn to Mary.

The hymn began with a long solo, and it was sung by the sweet voice of a girl, simply, beautifully, and piously as it should be in God's house. My aunt, who sat next to me in the small grated pew of the estate owner, noticed surely how I strained my gaze through the semidarkness over to the choir.

"Marianne, the Cantor's daughter," she whispered and then resumed praying with her rosary.

I had heard the most glorious church music over in Italy, but nothing had captivated me so before as this simple hymn to Mary from the Cantor's child. I could not sleep the entire night.

On the next morning, I set off on the path to the Cantor's house. I told my aunt I wanted to try out the organ, it had seemed not bad to me. —

The Cantor was an amiable man, just moving into the incipient stage of old age, his wife simply good-natured; but Marianne, for whom I had come, I did not see.

I brought up my request and found the friendliest accommodation. On the way to the church, the Cantor said, "In any case, my child, Marianne, is up there, she practises for an hour every morning."

"Your daughter, the little Miss, plays the organ!"

"She is no Miss, sir, just a simple child, but gentle and dear. She steps in sometimes for me, particularly in winter when it is cold."

I had wanted to say something polite about the previous day's hymn to Mary, but we were already entering the church. A gentle prelude sounded from the choir. I felt how my heart was pounding as we climbed up the narrow steps; the organ continued ringing out.

You find Saint Cecilia depicted thus. A gentle, clean profile; a delicate figure; heavy, blond plaits wound simply about the head; blue, sweet, dreamy eyes directed at the sheet music. I felt a feeling like devotion and love flood through my heart.

Now she became aware of us. With an abrupt blush, she broke off, sprang from the organ bench, and bowed her head gently, yet ashamed. I believe the Cantor whispered a few words, that I would be incapable of making any notes. The Cantor impelled me to the organ bench.

What I played first I do not know anymore, but I believe it was wild, discordant stuff. Then I calmed down, and played an old fugue. When it was over, I said it was enough for today and we should go.

When we had left the little church, I introduced myself to Marianne in all form as if to a great lady. She became very confused and seemed to me in this lovely confusion more charming than ever. Then the Cantor paid me a compliment over my organ playing. I disclaimed it laughing, and told then very earnestly of what a great impression the last hymn to Mary the day before had made on me; I then asked who sung it. Now Marianne answered.

"Do not mock, sir, I sung it myself, as we are just simply able to do it up here with us."

We started chatting, during which her shyness gradually faded away a little. I sat for a little while yet down in the school garden, then I gave my regards.

Like a dreamer, I stood in the village street. I did not know what had happened to me. But I felt one thing, just now not back to the castle, but to a right,

right simple little spot to be able to think! I walked for a piece through the forest, and came to the saw-mill. The water was rushing monotonously, the saws buzzing. That did me good. I laid myself down under a tree, and shut my eyes.

To start with, I thought of nothing at all, I could not think of anything. Then clear reflection came to me. I loved, loved a child who appeared to me with her pure heart like a saint; I was blessed. Yet then I was shocked to the depths of my heart. Was I permitted to love her, could then such a completely innocent soul ever join with another who in the storm of time and weakness had already suffered shipwrecks so often? Was that not a sacrilege? Thus from the beginning a fearful question merged into the jubilation of love in my heart.

But then the young, lovely luck which had struck my heart overcame me with completely unfamiliar bliss, and I could not torture myself with such dark images, I wanted to be happy and call her mine at any price.

A bird was singing a sweet song in the forest — the song of my love. I wanted to listen to it, but — the water was rushing monotonously, the saws were buzzing. It was unbearable, I plunged away, to home.

I saw her again, as a my love grew, so did my scruples vanish. I comforted myself with beautiful images. Must then the mariner, whose rocking boat roves about for a long time between storm and cliffs, and makes many a leak, when a fortunate wind drives him to the green isle of the blessed, must he not land there because his journey has not been smooth? Will he not forget the storm there in the safe port and be a calm man amongst calm men?

What wondrous philosophising the human heart does when it loves and desires! — —

Marianne saw in me still too much of the noble gentleman, and in herself the poor child, for me to be permitted to hope for a returned love. There music helped me.

The Cantor possessed a good Stainer violin. I played it often when I sat under the lime tree in the school garden with Marianne. I played at the time better than now, with far worse technique, but with much more soul.

How she listened, as if the notes were from a strange world of folktales which were incomprehensible to her. At the same time, she leant her blond head against the lime tree, and her blue eyes gazed into the distance as if she wanted to gaze at the strange thing which until then had been distant, far away from what could be sensed, but now came ever closer and closer with magical force to her, always to her.

And then the understanding came to her. It was one May evening, dreamy, mild, balmy, the bells were about to call to prayer. We were alone under the lime tree. I was playing the violin, I have surely never played so like that time. As the desire and love smouldered in my heart, they broke in passionate outpourings from the notes, and penetrated into her heart, begging and wooing. And then she understood me. The violin slipped from my hand. I gazed at her, she was crying bitterly.

I took her in my arms, she let it happen, and our lips found each other in a kiss.

The world was resting all around in the peace of evening. Golden clouds stood in the sky, and the bells tolled in our dream. — —

There was a second teacher in that place, a man who did not please me. He had a tall, doddery figure; his face was gaunt and yellow; his eyes cold and grey.

Above them the eyebrows had grown together. I rarely got together with him, he had almost always, however, a pointed remark. I considered him to be jealous; Marianne, on the contrary, was of the opinion that he was clever and at base good, if also sombre and repellent.

One Sunday I had played the organ. After the church service, I had come to the schoolhouse for an hour or so. The Cantor praised my playing as always. At the same time, there was a twitch about the corners of the other man's mouth — Günther was his name — something like mockery. I looked at him sharply.

"Don't take me wrong", he said, "but your organ playing does not please me. It should sound pious with you, and it doesn't; there is such a wrestling in it, a wrestling for peace and clarity, but you feel it will never obtain peace. There is a nasty passion there, which is surely breathed over by a pious note, but cannot be obscured. That may be great in a concert, but in the church, —".

I leapt up in fury.

"No harm meant", he said quite coolly and in an almost hearty tone, and left the room.

I was outraged; but when I wanted to lie down in bed that evening, I had not yet gotten over the bad words, and I tossed and turned the entire night sleeplessly with the anxious question, "Is he right? Is he right?" — —

Once more I met him. It had meanwhile turned into summer. I had once again gone back to the saw-mill. And again I lay under a tree to dream and meditate. There he stood suddenly before me.

"It's good that I meet you", he said, "I would like to talk with you alone for once."

"What subject endears you?"

He sat next to me without further ado.

"It concerns Marianne", he said quite calmly, "you think you love the child and will again —"

"Sir, what are you daring to suggest?", I flared up at him.

"I beg for a little bit of patience, afterwards you may say to me whatever you want. So, as I said, it is thus, and the Cantor is a fool and does not hinder it."

"You are impudent! Take care!"

"Please do not get excited, listen to me for Marianne's sake! You see, sir, it is all quite beautiful and idealistic, and I believe that you are heartily fond of the child, who wouldn't be; but, sir, what can come of it but misfortune, a great misfortune for the child? I mean it well, sir!"

"Your good opinion is absolutely out of order", I cried. "But now, since you are interfering for once, you may hear in God's name, yes, I love Marianne, and I think it will not be much longer before she is my wife."

"Yes, certainly," he nodded, "that is also all quite self-evident, but you see, sir, that is indeed the misfortune!"

"A misfortune", I laughed hard, "a misfortune at the most for you, as you are jealous!"

He remained calm, and just shook his head sadly.

"Which only you say, sir; I am just as little good for Marianne as you! She is like a flower, sir, a tender, individual flower, and she would have to die with either of us, with you from heat and with me from cold!"

"You are talking nonsense!"

"No nonsense, sir! Do you want to remain here, with us in the quiet valley? You could not, you have too hot a blood, and it forces out. Or do you want to take Marianne out there with you? Sir, do you not see then that it won't work? Don't you feel that Marianne with her simple ways would harvest nothing out in the big, cold, educated world but that secret mockery which she would surely feel and which would injure her heart? Would she then find a friendly heart in the circles in which she would enter with you?"

"You exaggerate, and even if it were so, she would have me", I responded uneasily.

"You, yes!", he said loudly. "Sir, it must come out! You see, you have a hot heart and will almost choke Marianne for a time with love. But then you will be desiring more than her; you will be unfaithful to her someday, sir, even if she is your wife, and then she will die!"

With a cry, I leapt up; it seemed to me as if I ought to murder him. Motionless and calm, with a deeply sad face, he sat before me. Then I ran off, half senseless.

From now on, my love had found a thorn. It overcame me in a seethingly hot way when Marianne came to talk about my past. How she imagined it though, the harmless child, cheerful, pure, peaceful as her own. She would always set the same measure against me as against herself, and I? — —

Visitors had arrived at the castle — distinguished summer visitors, also ladies. One was especially beautiful and witty. Hildegard was her name. She chatted wonderfully, knew how to delve into all my intentions with spirited charm and was full of the most affectionate coquetry. My love for Marianne, which did not remain hidden from her, she considered to be 'cute'. I hated the woman.

But she was very beautiful and a siren with a thousand spells, and I had such hot blood. One evening I had drunk a lot of champagne, and she had abstained from it — I kissed her. A few hour before, I had been with Marianne. — — —

How I survived the following night, I do not know. No hate, no enmity consumed my heart so much as hate and enmity towards myself. I believe I would have shot myself if I had not deemed the bullet too good for me. I raged against myself.

The next morning, I wrote a letter to Günther. I wrote to him that he was the greatest philosopher and I was the poorest devil I knew. After that my confession. He should tell her it.

I did not permit myself to see her anymore; nor to write to her. I meant to disavow her therewith.

Thus I moved away, in the morning hour. Great, heavy drops fell from the sky.

Günther wrote to me years later. She had become a nurse in the village. Her countenance remained pure and peaceful like that of an angel. She had become infected by a sick child, and had died. She had given me her regards.

But I have forced myself through storm and stress and hardship to a sort of peace which is only then truly pious and pure when I recall her." — —

My friend has finished. His head sinks down onto his hands. I sit for a while opposite him still, then I gently stroke his hot forehead and leave him alone. —

# WILTED LEAF

Outside the November storm is sweeping. It drives withered leaves down the village street and throws them menacingly at the windows of the human abodes. Most of all at those of the schoolhouse!

The man behind one window, standing and gazing at the desolate bustle, the schoolmaster, is an ancient man. Ancient, although he barely numbers sixty years. He has had to work a lot in his life, and has also had to bear much sorrow. For his work has bestowed little praise on him, and nobody has consoled him in his sorrows. But if you stand so alone and not a single soft hand caresses from the brow the furrows which affront and grief bury in the human countenance, then you will become old before your time. Very much before your time!

The old, surly housekeeper, Susanne, is not at home today. She is usually making a terrible amount of racket with her few pots and pans. Today it is quite still, and the schoolmaster can look undisturbed at the bustling of the November storm as it chases the withered leaves in the lane — up, down, in a mad whirl.

A verse occurs to the old man:

> Each year loyally brings
> Wilted leaves and wilted hopes.*

He is not sentimental — God preserve — but as he says the words to himself, he trembles lightly. A thought

---

\* From Nikolaus Lenau's *Herbstklage* (1831).

penetrates through his wrinkled forehead into his soul — he thinks of himself and of his life.

Young people do not believe in reminiscences. But the old in their many quiet hours also have the many quiet investigations of their conscience. Quite explicably! Anyone who stands before the settling of the account thinks of the balance; and anyone who has barely begun his account unconcernedly writes one entry after another.

A wind gust! It carries many wilted leaves with it.

Wilted leaves — wilted hopes!

His youth arises before the old man. His parents were deemed wealthy. But when his father died, it proved that people had been completely deceived.

He had to leave the elite high school which he was attending at the time. He had wanted to become a doctor, and now his first, beautiful blossom of hope had wilted. There was to be no more about "studies" anymore, he became a schoolmaster.

We must not do the old man an injustice. He did not belong to that good for nothing, elite high school junk who, entirely residual and unfit, consider themselves capable of stepping into a school subject, that is namely, to take on the education of the children of the nation. No, he was a gifted student.

An old man consoled him.

"My son, to be a doctor is a beautiful profession, to be a teacher a more beautiful one. Or don't you think that it would be something greater to awaken a slumbering human soul to a beautiful life than to patch up a sick, broken body to make it weather-fast for yet another year?"

The seventeen year old did not understand it rightly. But it was spoken beautifully, the more so as the man who said it was himself a doctor. Later the meaning of those words was grasped by the inspired schoolmaster.

## Wilted Leaf

How he worked, how he struggled with his fervent efforts against crudity and ignorance his whole life long! And when he dismissed the children, when he sent them well-behaved and good into their life, then he folded his hands for the prayer, "God protect my seed!"

But when he heard a few years later the same children as adolescent factory boys and girls making a racket down the village street, then it gave him a stab in the heart. —

Wilted leaf! —

It was always very lonely. He had accustomed himself to it, and hardly believed surely that it would ever be any different. Then love came into his heart, pure and great, and the loneliness became a torment to him. It now drew him powerfully to *her*.

On the edge of the forest stood her house. — It was a wonderful, lovely September evening. The light forest stood in a profusion of colour about a lonely meadow, on it a few deer were grazing. It was all so beautiful without measure, and peaceful and uplifting. And she sat before him on the green garden bench in her sweet beauty.

That day he had to tell her. And then, when she became his, then it would become light in the constricted schoolhouse, then — there a shock passes through his limbs. If she spurns him! He is a poor man and 15 years older than her. Yet the victorious hope returns. He dares it.

"Marianne", he begins, and a hot wave floods through his heart, "Marianne —".

Then a friendly greeting disturbs him from the garden fence. The young hunter it is; he is bringing her a bouquet of flowers.

She leaps up. Her face glows lovingly, and a radiance breaks from her blue eyes — the radiance of love.

Paul Keller

The schoolmaster caught the radiance. It hurt him in the chest; the young flower of his love died. The evening wind rises, and passes gently through the trees ... Wilted leaf! ...

At her wedding, he played the organ, and a year afterwards, when she had died, also at her funeral. It was the schoolmaster's duty. —

His life now became yet quieter. He performed his work, but without lively interest. The best teachers are mostly the happy ones. And he was very unhappy.

Then "her" child came to his school. At the beginning, he observed her with a hostile look; for her sake "she" had indeed had to die. But then he became fond of little Marianne. She had the blue eyes of her mother and her sweet, dear manner. Thus she became the child of his love, and his best teaching charge.

He began now to study again — for Marianne's sake. He paid attention to every stirring in the child's intellect and disposition; he made notes about her, worked them up into psychological sketches, and sought incessantly for the best means and ways of developing Marianne's talents to be the most brilliant. What a poignant imagination he developed, how original and how good as well were his educational methods!

The entire village was proud of Marianne, most of all certainly he who educated her. Often, when he saw her quiet, unhurried actions, his eyes became moist. Then he thought always of his dead love. And wondrously, his soul remained free of anguish. The love had remained, it had rejuvenated itself, yet the anguished desire had faded away; it had become still in him, he was happy. And then again the soul of the teacher in him stirred, and he enjoyed the great, ideal joy of a visibly God-blessed teaching work. Heaven gives every life *one* gift of grace; his life's gift of grace was Marianne.

His Marianne, his pride, his love!

# Wilted Leaf

And yet she, the original picture of innocence and a simple heart, had not remained spared from the odious drooling tongue of sneering distrust. She was now 20 years old, a magnificently blossomed child, and kept house for her father, the Count's forester.

The son of the Count sometimes came to the house of the forester's — of course, he had to negotiate with the forester. And if he spoke a few words with Marianne at the same time, what did that do to her, what did that do to his Marianne?!

And that infamous rogue, that village councillor, dared to say *that* to him? — That? — Of his Marianne? It had been on the street when he hissed it to him, and then he had punched him in in the middle of the face so that he staggered. The councillor had indicted him, and he was convicted. It may be that he was advocating for his Marianne, and if he was sent to prison for it. —

Again a wind gust! A hail of withered leaves smashes against the window. The old man starts heftily. Suddenly he stands quite still ... as if spellbound.

There the front door opens. It falls back hard again into its lock straightaway. By the wind?

Now old Suzanne plunges into the room. She looks horrific — like calamity itself. Her face is chalk white, her eyes are frightfully large, her grey hair has been released by the wind and tossed about her gaunt shoulders.

"Jesus, Maria — it is true — what the people — say — about — Marianne, — she — she — they have — found — her — just now — in the mill pool!"

The old schoolmaster stands as if struck by lightning. His eyes protrude glassily from their sockets; his hands grasp in the air, a strange slurring sounds brokenly from his mouth, "Ma — ri — a —."

He sways two steps towards the door, then he sinks to the ground — dead —.

## Paul Keller

Outside, the November storm is sweeping. It drives withered leaves down the village street, and throws them menacingly at the windows of the human abodes. Most of all at those of the schoolhouse!

# A SPRINGTIME FOLKTALE

The wellspring becomes bored in the hollows of the mountain. There are few amusements down there, and bad company. A fat stone lies in a soft depression, and sleeps and turns over to the other side barely once in ten years, and a little red sand is there which is capable of flirting quite well in summer with favourable light, but in winter is almost just as boring as the stone. And now it is winter. The wellspring looks through crystalline, little, ice windows up above, and a gulp swells up from it, which sounds like a sigh.

"If only it were spring!"

The old oak which stands near the wellspring heard that, and had sympathy with the little, impatient thing at its feet. It inclined its top thus, and whispered down, "Just wait a little while; spring is coming soon; I sense it already in all my limbs!"

Thus old people are almost always right, especially in reference to the weather. So spring came then too after three or four days. The March sun seemed warm through the branches of the forest, and thawed a round hole in the little window of the wellspring. — It also straightaway began to chatter, the lively thing, "Good morning Mr Oaktree!"

"Good morning, young Miss Wellspring! Well, lively already?"

"Eh yes, Mr Oaktree, but not already, rather finally! It is not nice at all down there, nothing at all to laugh at, to chat, to skip, to tease! There you have it much better, Mr Oaktree, stretching your head so high into the clouds and being able to gaze as far as you want!"

"Hm, have not seen anything special either, up here!"

"But you were free though, and I was locked in! Oh, what good this open air does! I want though to straight-away go a little down into the valley; I believe I'll forget the way otherwise! I am really in a great hurry, Mr Oak-tree —".

"Gently, gently, little Miss, stay a little up here! You could sprain your little ankles going down, for you would have a quite nasty path. The little brook hangs down still over the mountain like a frozen rope, and at the waterfall you could fall to your death on the ice floes."

"Eh, but Mr Oaktree!"

"Don't pout, little thing, it must ensue! And is it so bad up here then? Can you not while away a little time and tell me some tale?"

"Tell a tale, eh, that will work! Telling a tale is good!", the slightly appeased, little wellspring answered, and began telling. — What did it tell? Eh now, almost utterly silly stuff; how should such a little thing know anything sensible?

It told of the little, silver fish which reside under the alders and which it feeds, of a young, beautiful lime tree which stands on the bank, and which threw it scented blossom the previous year, of a surly juniper cane which it tickles on the roots, but which does not want to make a friendly face, of a little beetle which sails in a golden coat on a green leaf across the water, of the little water-mill which turns so lustily and which it once put to shame, of a thirsty little bullock in whose nose it sprayed water so that it puffed loudly and had to sneeze, and more such things which only a little stream can experience.

The oak listened like an affectionate grandpa who is chattered to somewhat enthusiastically by a little granddaughter. "You have always been an amusing thing", he praised her, "and can tell lots; certainly you also have a course which is almost an hour long."

"Yes, if you don't run too quick, almost a full hour", the little wellspring said eagerly, "and if the stupid ditch and then the great river did not come, then I would run all the way to the sea. But so —".

"Don't get excited, little Wellspring, you get about widely enough! Think of me! I am now nearly 400 years old, and am still standing on the same spot at which a jay placed the acorn from which I grew. You can believe it, even if I have been gazing almost 400 years always in the same direction, I can though see something new every day; you just have to have good eyes. But don't you pout! Instead tell me something more! Do you know nothing from the school?"

"Oh — eh — from the school", the little wellspring said in a long drawn out way; "nothing good, Mr Oaktree, nothing good!"

"I thought so", the tree nodded sadly.

"You thought so?", the little wellspring asked.

"Yes, I saw him walking past once in winter. You know, the young schoolteacher. I certainly did not know what he wanted up here, but I saw that he was making a very sombre face."

"Oh — eh — yeah", the little wellspring said, "he has been making a sombre face for a long time! It was sad down there last autumn."

"Tell, little Wellspring, tell!"

"You knew, Mr Oaktree, how cheerful he always was! No path was too bad for him, and no water too cold, even came up here once. And he never walked past us both. He always leant on your trunk, and I believe he knew every fold in your venerable coat. He had less respect for me. He sprang away over me, that might yet be okay, but he often placed his foot in my course so that I could not continue, and that was irksome. But it was fun when he skipped little stones over me; then I laughed teasingly with every throw, and he laughed along. Think though, Mr Oaktree, anyone who annoys a wellspring and can then laugh again with it straight afterwards, he is a good man."

"And a happy one", the oak tree added.

"Oh — eh — yeah", the little wellspring sighed. "He was happy; but isn't anymore! You know my course, Mr Oaktree, can gaze far from me, far, almost to the stupid ditch, and you thus also know that I flow close past the schoolhouse. It is quite splendid, down there! First comes a meadow, then a garden; in the garden is a little gully, and in the little gully am I. To the right of the gully, there are in spring marsh-marigolds — yellow, Mr Oaktree — and to the left are the forget-me-nots — blue, Mr Oaktree! Yellow and blue and me silvery white in the middle, you should see that sometime! But it gets even better! There is a little stone trough there — I come to the trough, and — hey! — it goes down in silvery arcs. The trough has filled up! That can't happen any different, for I have water enough; and so I run past, that is, I clamber down the stone wall again, and run onwards. But it gets even better.

In the schoolyard there is a well into which a squeaking pipe is stuck. When you pull on the pipe, water comes out. But quite suddenly, and thick and rumbling, Mr Oaktree! It can hardly taste good either; for don't think that one of the schoolchildren goes to the well to drink! All prefer to come to me, and the boys press their red, fat cheeks to the trough and suck up a mouthful, and the girls hold their cupped hands under, fine and decent, there where I run over, and the boys smack the water in the trough so that it sprays up high, and the girls get wet and run away from there squealing — is that not a delight, Mr Oaktree?

You see, and the schoolteacher always liked watching, what with the boys and the girls and me, for he was cheerful, and liked listening to the children laugh and to me splashing. All at once everything changed! Suddenly the children were not permitted to tease each other anymore at the trough, often hard words resounded from the schoolroom, into which children's crying was mixed, and when a bird sang on the window sill, the window slammed shut quickly and loudly. And all that since the day when he had been up here, with the girl who wore such a beautiful dress and spoke so cleverly and laughed so quietly, not like any girl up here ever does."

"I know", the oak said; "they sat together at my feet and were surely two beautiful humans. But I did not feel good about it at all."

"Did you know what they talked about?"

"Hm, an oak tree has a good memory. I noted every word."

"Then tell me; I am almost always forgetting again."

"I don't like telling about it; for it did not please me much at all at the time. But it involves you as much as me, and so I would like to oblige you, since you have forgotten. — She was a pale girl from the town and came here to redden her cheeks like many other people also do. It is not good, little Wellspring, that now so many strangers are always down there in the valley. It makes so much of a racket where before it had been quite still with us. I have had bleak experiences. Once a young couple came up here, and they spoke much of love and loyalty. He took a knife and cut a heart and two letters into my bark. Fourteen days afterwards, they both walked past one another as if they did not like to recognise each other, and yet both had laughing faces. For an old tree like me, however, the heart burns in my bark like a mark of shame. So I was shocked when I saw him with a stranger, for I was fond of him, the young school-teacher, and I suspected no good. They sat on the grass at my feet, and leant against my trunk. They did not speak for a long time; then he seized her hand. His voice quivered when he said, 'I don't have money or property, and don't possess any high office; but I am not poor! — How happy I always am in spring! Then the trees before my windows flower and like to stretch branches full of blossoms right to me in the quiet schoolhouse; then the birds sing, the flowers give off their scent, and my heart expands, and the children's eyes before me begin to gleam and to light up so brightly, so clearly, and as blue as the bright sky outside. And when in the evenings the stars pass over our quiet village, and a silvery light weaves about the little church and my own quiet her-mitage, then it seems to me as if peace resides with me. Is that not a fortune which is capable of transforming life? Is a beautiful home, a noble office, and a heart which has its peace really balanced out more by a hand full of silver and by the loud tumult which you call vari-ety and commerce? Could you not be happy with me in this valley; is this teacher's life really too poor for you?'

His cheeks glowed when he spoke thus, and his eyes hung on her lips. Then she spoke, and her words soun-ded calm and clever and cold, 'You are a nature oriented towards ideals, that makes you interesting; but your idealism goes far too far! What you say about the blos-soms, about the birds, and about the lighting up in the eyes of your children, that all sounds quite beautiful, but it is not real, not tangible fortune. Such a thing warms the heart in a mellow hour, but it is also only an hour, you hear, an hour, and such an hour has only sixty minutes.'

He looked at her in shock.

'Yes, but the purity of such a feeling of happiness and the after-effects of such an hour!'

'Listen now', she continued; 'your home is beautiful, without any question, but it offers every day the same charms, and it must thus deaden the soul towards them. I would not be capable of recognising this beauty for longer than a few weeks; then boredom would seize me. And I am a woman! How though could you as a man find satisfaction in the stillness of this valley! Oh, you do not know how magnificent, how exciting it is to listen to the heartbeat of the big wide world! It races, it falters, it seethes, it surges, it twitches in all the whirlings of passion, it struggles and wrestles, floods always forwards, is eternally different, and never stands still! No, my friend, I am not made to be happy in such a narrow valley!'

She fell silent, and he let go of her hand. I felt how he trembled all over. He opened his eyes wide, and gazed down into the valley of his home. The evening gold lay on the simple cottages, and the schoolhouse sent up its greetings from the green of the lime tree. Then he trembled more vehemently. He passed his hand caressingly over my rough bark, and also looked at you, little Wellspring. But then he burst out, hastily and quickly, 'I am very fond of you and will endeavour to obtain myself a position in the big city!'

'That is sensible', the other person said, 'and now we can continue talking. Yes, it shall soon become quite clear between us! It is not only the place in which you live which would make it impossible for me to be happy with you, there is yet something else again — your profession!'

Then he started and suddenly stood erect before her.

'Adelheid! What are you doing! You are wounding my heart when you vilify my profession! Oh, you were not serious, you cannot have been serious! No, no, certainly not! What more noble a profession could there be than that which ignites lights in dark human souls, strengthens and emboldens weak hearts, and shows swaying children's feet the way to their salvation? None, none!'

She smiled. 'You are just an enthusiast! When you translate your words into simple, true prose, it sounds quite different. What does your office consist of? You attempt to break the worst habits of farming children, but habits into which they always fall back again because the just as unpolished parents at home are the stronger instructors. Onward! You arduously teach the children a few pitiful bits of knowledge which they have, however, again forgotten as soon as they have been two years out of school. What then is high and beautiful in this profession whose success, far more than is the case in other positions, conflicts with the amount of hassle, privation, and disrespect which comes to those who practise it? Yes, keep glaring at me with your eyes, at the disrespect, I say, for if it might be somewhat better here in the countryside, with us in the city every number summing secretary counts, every —'

'Stop, Adelheid, you have no heart! And even if it were all true, what you describe there far too darkly, if the teaching profession really were the last and most despised post, then would not the one who endures in this post despite hunger and work and contempt, because he believes in having to endure for the sake of a higher good, would he not be a noble man who deserves his little portion of love? Adelheid, do not ask that I abandon this post!'

'And yet I must ask it, for I am incapable of placing myself in your position, I am not capable of becoming the wife of a teacher. You will surely say that love sacrifices; well now, why don't you bring me a sacrifice which certainly seems difficult to you, but which only frees you of a burden which you would feel as such sooner or later. You possess a good, poetic power, ample enough to achieve something great. Do not waste it any further in beautiful but wasteful trivialities! Make your name well-known so that I want to be yours!'

'That is a phantom, Adelheid, a phantom!'

'But I believe in it, and if you also believe in it, the phantom will become reality; the belief in your own powers works wonders. Go for the time-being into the big city as a teacher, seek excitement there, seek connections. Your talent will forge a path. I am not exactly thinking of a modern dramatist, but if you just have a respected name and perhaps a position in a good editorial office, then I will be yours.'

'Adelheid, I cannot! I can abandon my home; but I am too fond of my profession!'

'Then let us part without ill will!'

She stood up and offered him her hand. The evening sun wove a gilded wreath about her hair; she was so beautiful at this moment. The poor schoolteacher looked at the lovely apparition which wanted to part from him. Then all the blood surged into his heart, and he burst out, 'I — will — do everything — that — you want!'

They slowly descended the mountain; she spoke animatedly to him, but he kept his head lowered. He had that day betrayed his home and profession, and she was the victor.

Behind my trunk, a quiet weeping sounded. There the forester's lovely daughter sat, who had heard everything. You surely know, little Wellspring, what made the poor child's heart heavy. She often sat up here, and gazed down at the schoolhouse. Was fond of him, him down there!"

The oak fell silent, but the wellspring sobbed loudly, "Oh, what a sad story that is! Now he will become unhappy, and the poor forester's child too. It will surely also all come about, he has not come here a single time anymore!"

"Will be ashamed, little Wellspring, for us!"

"Yes, yes, ashamed", the little Wellspring repeated and sobbed quietly to itself. And with all its sobbing, it fell asleep. A cold evening wind passed through the forest and drew a thin sheet of ice over the little stream again. —

***

Barely ten steps from the oak stood an old pine. A man had leant on its trunk the entire time, and heard everything which the oak tree and the wellspring said. He had listened quite attentively, for they both spoke about him. — Now he went home.

On the forest path, just where it joined the village street, he met a child. The child scurried past him with a hurried greeting. Usually it would have been different, the children had always hurried joyfully to him when they had met him on the street. But in the past while, he had always had so much to think about that he had become nervous, and at school there had been many bad canings. Hence, the little ones now avoided him. At this moment, it seemed to him as if he were losing something. Would he find it again?

"The town children have too many teachers, they will not be so devoted", he opined in walking onwards. —

A poor labourer comes, then a rich farmer. Both greet him.

"Just how will it be in the city?", he thinks. —

Now he comes to the little church. It sits so wonderfully peaceful in the middle of the little churchyard so that you must pray when you merely see it from outside.

He was once in a cathedral. There was a quite solemn service there, and very beautiful music; but he could not pray a single "Our Father". The many people pressed against each other and stepped on each others feet. — —

Now he is at the schoolhouse. He pauses. "If I were a painter", he thinks, "I would paint it. There was seldom a house that sits so beautifully as this one, and certainly none that I am so fond of. I would take the picture with me and hang it in my new room."

At that the question occurred to him of where he will live in the big city. "On the third floor of a large house — well yes!"

He looked again and again at the charming cottage, and once he had to wipe his hand over his forehead. At the front door, he turns to the right. He wants to gaze once into the garden to see if the snowdrops are already blooming. They are indeed for him! When the carnations bloom, and the lilies and roses, he will already be far away — in the big city to make his fortune. — The snowbells were already blooming, and the wind was swinging their light bells. How beautiful it is! —

He stands unexpectedly by the little trough which the little wellspring told of. He looks thoughtfully at the shining ice. A short distance away from it, there is an old willow.

What the twilight does! The old willow takes on human forms. It looks just like a gypsy woman who can tell the future. And — is it the night wind, or does what rings in his ears really sound from over there?

"Sleep, little stream, sleep! You will soon flow again, and run day after day. Then you will see a stranger standing by your mirror. And the other one whom you know will be far away. But someday — how long will it be? — your water will run into the great current, there you will see a weary man standing on the banks, a man whom you know. He will be exhausted by misfortune, worn down by disappointment, and betrayed by false love! Little stream, will you then still sing him a comforting song from his home?"

The dreamer by the water trough starts abruptly. He turns around, and flees. Inside in his room, he sits for a long time. —

"Why does this love lay so much winter ice on top of my heart? Was it a love at all, or was it just a deceptive excitation? If I could change it!"

He struggles and struggles; then he says, "She has my word! I will not cover over any stain on my honour!"

On the table lie three letters which he only now notices. — He opens the first letter. An important newspaper has accepted his first longer work. He barely smiles. — He opens the second letter. The summoning to the big city! He begins to tremble heftily. — And now the third letter. — It contains her rejection of him.

A loud cry — he collapses in a faint. On his pale face lies the shimmer — of salvation. —

\*\*\*

"Good morning, Mr Oaktree!"

"Good morning, Miss Wellspring!"

"Today I am quite definitely going down though, Mr Oaktree, you must not take that the wrong way! I dreamt something beautiful last night about yellow willow catkins and green tips of grass. I also saw daisies and snowbells. Do you not also hear how the sparrows are making a racket? That has to mean something! Hey, Mr Oaktree — spring, spring! So make a friendly face now though and forget the old tales which can't be changed. And now adieu, Mr —".

"Stop, little Miss, just for a little while, someone is coming through the forest!"

It was the young teacher. He leant his head against the oak's trunk, and a few pale drops flowed through the furrows of its bark.

# A Springtime Folktale

"I am not leaving you, not ever, not ever! My fortune is with you, how could I find it out there?"

Then he stepped to the wellspring, and became more cheerful.

"Little wellspring, you can do me a pleasure! You go far, even to the big city! And here are three letters which I have no use for. Would you like to carry these to the big city from which they came?"

"Oh — eh — yes — yes — very much", the little wellspring exulted.

Then the young teacher took the three letters, tore them up and strew the little pieces into the stream. It bubbled up brightly, and leapt down into the valley with the little pieces of paper. But the spring wind passed through the old oak with a mighty roar.

The young teacher stood for a long time yet in the same place. With radiant eyes, he gazed down at his home valley. And for once he looked also for a long time up the path which led to the forester's house.

And right at this moment, it was at its mightiest in him — the feeling of the coming of spring. — —

# POOR CHILDREN

Counted exactly, I have three poor students. That is more than enough for a teacher, for poor children are quite difficult to handle properly. I have just today ruined the afternoon mood by the reading of a squalid story in which much of the talk was of a boy through whose clothes at individual spots the autumn wind shall have whistled, who had to rub his cold, blue fingers warm, and in the evening found in a thatched cottage only a piece of black bread for supper. This boy was meant to be "poor", and was for this reason commiserated with quite touchingly by the author. The writer had, by the composition of his output, certainly not the slightest idea of the nature of poverty; I can claim this all the more calmly and definitely, as I have myself, years ago, unfortunately written the sort of thing which brought about the mood with the reading today. I was at the time still very young, that is my only excuse.

There is hardly anything more needless than sentimentality, and certainly no feeling with which such a monstrous amount of rubbish is spawned as with pity. How much strength has gone to rot at the first budding because awkward, sinful pity hinders fate from awakening it; how many a shoulder, strong enough to bear burdens or to learn to bear burdens, has been pressed lamely to the crutch onto which helpful strangers pressed them! How distant sentimental pity is from the

Christian ideal, from compassion, as distant as a squalid titillation of a weak disposition must be distant from the high, holy virtue of a strong soul.

Poor children! It would be awful if every boy who came to school barefoot in summer and in clattering wooden clogs in winter were a poor child. When the child is healthy, he will in summer as in winter make his lusty leaps, perhaps higher than the "rich" comrade who wears beach shoes in July and fur-lined boots from the middle of October, and any stupid thought will come to the boy rather than that he is poor. Most men thus only feel poor because it is made plausible to them in some way, for poverty hardly depends on something so little as on the non-possession of temporal goods. When you follow up the evidence of the "poor" boy's life course, he will seem to you to be a lusty fellow up until leaving school, later you can hear him as a labourer whistling extremely contentedly behind his plough, and if you have the fortune of being a cantor or sexton, you can play for him, the happy bridegroom, the wedding march, and later see him now and again ordering the christening with an amiably bashful grin. Is this man poor?

If you then want to count poor children, do not by any means count scanty, children's clothes — your example would not at all tally up then. And yet there are poor children enough. From their great number, I want to select just three examples and would like to number these thus: 1. the sick, 2. the ugly, and 3. the beggarly poor child.

# 1. The Sick Child

In my schoolroom, there is a place for needs of the saddest sort. There in a wheelchair, wrapped well in soft blankets, sits a pale, perhaps twelve year old boy, Franz Stiller, the son of a farmer. The poor boy has such weak, sick legs that he is unable to run for a step; his upper body by contrast is quite normal. Now and again, a doctor has received a lot of money, but Franz has remained sitting in his chair, and will surely also remain seated there his entire life long.

To his misfortune, the boy has a bold, ardent heart. What he does not suffer in, for example, a history lesson. I cannot and must not stop myself from being lively in my descriptions, from describing heroes who, with courage, physical strength, and dexterity, achieve great things. Then Franz sits with burning cheeks in his wheelchair, his heart beats harder, his arms twitch, his upper body bends forward as if he straining out from under his blankets, and when the lesson is over, the beautiful thrill must fly away, the poor boy feels that he will never be capable of achieving similar things, although his heart yearns so much after them.

It is similar in the quarter hour breaks. The other boys run, leap, tumble, test their strength, and each one feels he is a hero. Franz sits in the sun and watches. And yet it urges him also to activation of strength.

Two small incidents really shocked me. Once I saw another boy standing by Franz's wheelchair, and pull and tear at his hand. When I moved over quickly, Franz called to me with shining eyes and voice trembling with delight, "I have a pfennig in my hand. If he can open the hand, he gets it! But he won't get it! Oh, I am strong!" —

And another time, I asked him what he wanted to get for Christmas. There he said, "I would like most of all a rolling hoop, but —".

And he cried.

Poor boy! He is a Prometheus in the small, has a bold heart, full of plans and impatient urge to action, and is yet shackled and exposed to the vultures, to the vultures of illness.

Who pities the poor boy? The parents expend love in their way and — lament. That is heartily little. The boy will never be happy, because his suffering is incurable. Nevertheless, something must happen which rescues his soul from embittering. It must, "schoolmaster", do you hear? Rack your brain and create a way out!

I brood, brood, and think over the situation. Every man seeks something which fills out his life; when he finds this, he is happy; when he does not find it, he must become a great philosopher, a great sceptic, or a — great sleepyhead, if it should not weigh him down. Franz is none of the three. He also seeks something which will satisfy him, and his yearning goes towards the activation of physical power. That is an easily explicable fact, yes, it is self-evident. For one, Franz acts like all men, he yearns for that which he cannot have, and secondly, he lives in the countryside, where physical strength is deemed by far the most important thing, and this thus floats constantly before the boy as an ideal. But should Franz ever desire an inner contentment which is capable of approximately balancing his outer misery, then he must seek this in the intellectual realm.

My task will thus be to guide the boy's creative urge, his yearning for the development of strength from the physical over to the intellectual side, and then, when the way has been started, distance the boy from the village.

There is certainly more than enough to do there. The interests of the boy cannot suddenly be given a different direction, a transition must be created, and indeed as pleasantly as possible.

Then the thought comes to me of gifting the boy a chessboard, and of introducing him to the art of playing chess. Success teaches me that I have struck the right path. The boy plays chess with a true passion, on the face of it certainly only because it concerns a game of combat, and he imagines a battle between each party, in which victory must be won with difficulty. I pursue my ideas unseen by him though. Franz gradually realises that the player's good thought is more important than the strongest figure, and by and by I teach him that in proper war the many thousands of soldiers with their strong arms and legs are also only figures which, well used, work well, but that far more important than them is the commander who leads them all, and that the latter does not require great physical strength, but rather higher intellectual gifts, yes, that there were famous commanders who were physically abject. There the boy listens up, and for the first time, he becomes conscious of the infinite superiority of intellectual strength over robust force.

Like a hot wave of blood, the happiness in this knowledge strikes into his young heart, he cries exuberantly in his naive way, "Ah — I — also want to be such an invalid commander!"

I teach him further that heroism is not only to be found on the battlefield, that there are victories, high, sweet victories which are yet more difficult to obtain than a success by cannons, and I win over the soul of this child, ignite in him fiery zeal for intellectual work.

Franz has a glorious talent for drawing and painting. I have tried to explain everything to his father; he has understood none of it, but as I absolutely insisted that Franz must go to the town for training, he said, "Then he may, because you want it, for you are very fond of him."

I certainly was very fond of him, he is so poor! I leave it to God that the last part of my calculations also proves itself correct! — —

# 2. The Conspicuously Ugly Child

I want to be honest — I feel, as probably all men tend to feel, that I would rather look at a pretty girl than an ugly one. (Unfortunately I am so vile as to at least suppose in parentheses that with a considerable part of the fairer sex the opposite is often the case.) Since I am now, however, not a young lady, a pretty face is thus also for me near to a letter of candidacy for my sympathies. That is admittedly just as little clever as fair, and is at most weakly excused by the famed sense for beauty. Fortunately, the cool, balanced understanding always soon returns to you if you carry a piece of honest sentiment in your heart, and then the beautiful letter of recommendation becomes for you at most enormously incidental. Thus what becomes occasionally difficult for me in life comes quite easily to me in the school.

I have an extraordinarily ugly girl student whom I nevertheless or rather directly as a result am very fond of. She is called Charlotte, and is the daughter of our head forester. For this unfortunate child, everything is askew — her figure, her head, her mouth, her eyes, yes, even the fingers on her hands. That is no exaggeration, nature is just as often an appalling stepmother.

# Poor Children

Charlotte has two "pretty" sisters, who are both in a boarding school; she herself shall "only" be taught by me. That "only" stems from the charming mouth of the head forester's wife. It did not affront me at the time at all, for I know the boarding school wisdom and know the head forester's wife, but it does stick in my heart though for Charlotte's sake. Charlotte is not only a stepchild by nature, but also a stepchild of her own mother; she is neglected, neglected in every way, because she is ugly.

Hapless mother, what shall I call you? Actually I yearn to call you abysmally bad; but I want to exercise lenience with your boundless vanity, and consider you just to be extraordinarily stupid.

Yet today I am outraged when I think of last Christmas Eve. I was at the head forester's place for the distribution of presents. Both the young ladies at boarding school were so amply furnished that I now do not wonder anymore over why the head forester always goes about so comparatively shabbily. It all goes west on outward frills for the wife and the two daughters. And Charlotte?

Her little Christmas table was eviscerated next to the heavily laden tables of her sisters, as if presents were being distributed there to a goose maid. A few practical things and nothing else, no object of luxury, none of the exciting thousands of superfluous things which simply delight a child's heart.

She stood by the flannel material which belonged to the absolutely necessary dress, and plucked with her hand at it; she also looked at the winter shoes which she needed, and the indispensable hat, but no shimmer of joy flew over her face. Only when mama, who stood for an eternity by the other girls, asked her incidentally whether she was pleased, did she smile obediently, and say, "Yes, mother, very much!"

That was a lie, my child, but God will let it atone for another — your mother!

I was at the time engaged, and had bought that afternoon for my fiancee a little, golden heart like those that ladies tend to wear about their necks. Luckily I had that with me. With quick resolve, I reached into my pocket.

"Here, Charlotte, the baby Jesus also sent something through me, a little, golden heart because you yourself have a little heart of gold, and because I am very fond of you."

There a trembling passed over the ugly child's figure. Then she flung her arms about me with a cry of joy, and cried, cried with anguish and with joy. The head forester's wife gave me a grim look. That I endured steadfastly.

A few days afterwards, a similar scene. A forestry advisor had come for an audit, and had returned afterwards to the head forester's house. Why I was called in for the dinner, I do not know, enough that I was present. Both boarding school girls paraded in new dresses. I considered them to be entirely lacking in taste, which was not saying much admittedly. Worse was that both young ladies also tried to impress the forestry advisor in another way. They waffled on in a sinful French yet more sinful nonsense. The forestry advisor was gallant, and merely smiled. After the dinner, he said to the lady of the house, "I believe I heard you had three daughters."

Charlotte was "of course" not with them at dinner. Now, however, the head forester's wife became quite embarrassed, and stuttered, quite in contrast to her usual flowing talk, "Yes — admittedly — the child — she is — not here."

Then I could not hold myself any longer.

"Charlotte, the youngest, is my student. She is working on an essay upstairs. — May I fetch her, madam?"

# Poor Children

A wrathful look, then she smiled like goodness itself. "If you will be so kind."

I was so kind, and went, even went very quickly so as not to be witness to the repellent scene of how the head forester's wife apologised to the forestry advisor on behalf of the unfortunate child, as if she were confessing to a crime.

The forestry advisor was a sensible man. He slung an arm around Charlotte, stroked her, and chatted with her. The child's eyes lit up, and the head forester's wife breathed deeply. But I went home deeply enraged.

I paced my room restlessly. The life's fortune of my student stood before my eyes. How poor this child is! What shook her in the first hour of her existence as a heavy misfortune, she will be made to feel her whole life long as if it were a proscriptive guilt.

Her need for love will increase with the years. Suitors will come to the house, her sisters will be loved, will be admired, they will dazzle and exult and sing, and she will have to gaze at this blessedness from a distance.

Occasionally she will be called in to the festivities, and just those will be her bitterest hours. A miserable person is astute. She sees the quiet shock which twitches over the faces of strangers at the first encounter, she hears the forced note in the conversation, and she feels deeply, even if she is quite modest, the pain in her young heart when she is always, always the last to play and dance, perhaps is even only tolerated as an unavoidable evil.

No blessedness of children, no love, no wedded bliss, no motherhood, what is the woman then!

Be merciful, "schoolmaster", you don't have much, but what you have, dedicate to this poor child!

Do you know the way? Love the child, love it so much that it believes in love! A human who has once in life felt love cannot be entirely embittered. And then ensure

Paul Keller

that her soul remains beautiful, and becomes still more beautiful! There is no consciousness of the innate beauty of the soul, but there is a sweet, holy divining of it. That is peace!

And exercise the compassion of this child! If thankful lips tilt to the hands of this poor child, then her poverty will at that moment stop, she will be rich.

# 3. The Beggarly Poor Child

Karl has neither father nor mother. The mother died soon after his birth, and the father —. It is very bad when a child has no completely proper name. How often must he blush, blush as a result, because he is in the world.

But that is not all. Karl is the grandchild of the beggar Trine. The beggar Trine lives in a sort of ruin at the end of the village, and she herself is also a ruin, old, frail, ugly, and useless like the old house.

The beggar Trine has her life long never led a joyful existence. Impoverished, frustrated, hidden, she has sat often and for a long time in prisons. Since time immemorial she has been a burden on the parish, particularly since she cannot work anymore because of her contorted fingers. She had already moved with her child into the village many years ago, long before I came to the village. She carried in a dirty rag the still dirtier nursling, and went begging from farm to farm. The farmers gave her a gift, mocked her occasionally, or threatened her sometimes with the dogs, depending on their mood. The pond builder behaved most vilely of all, and yet — —. There are many sins in the world!

The daughter of the beggar Trine grew up, and she became the mother of my current student, Karl. Then she died.

Karl is a miserable boy. The rags hang about his body wantonly to the highest degree, and they are extraordinarily bad for him just because he seems to fit into them so. There are people who in rags embody a peculiar beauty. But here an emaciated, ugly figure; a shy, depressed being who feels unspeakably weak and whose instinct mutters nothing about his human dignity to him. He always stands apart, mostly with lowered head, just as if he had a bad conscience. The other children despise him, and he considers this derision to be something quite understandable, to be something which does not unfortunately, does not at all unfortunately aggrieve him, but rather pushes him away timidly into the corner.

Just as he puts up with everything from everyone, so does he beg from everyone. He begs for everything possible. When his request is not granted, he begs for something else. Yes, he lets himself be joshed, pushed, hit, and mistreated by the other boys for a gift. And that is actually all quite understandable. I often put myself — every teacher must — mentally in the position of my students, also in the position of Karl, and then I find that I would under his life circumstances stand just as pitifully in the corner as he does. I do not use this exercise as a means against my pride, which is not great anyway, but so that I am put in the place to judge and treat Karl fairly.

I am unendingly sorry for the poor boy, not so much because he must often go without what is necessary, but rather because the consciousness of human dignity, which usually resides instinctively in every human, is suppressed in him. His soul has in a way a broken back, it can never assume a strapping pose, an expression of willpower is impossible for it, it collapses into itself.

You must, "schoolmaster", help find a prescription, or must at least honestly attempt to!

I have ransacked and referred to a few psychological theories which are recommended by the wisest gentlemen as means for the strengthening of self-confidence. I have rejoiced that the people write in such a pretty style. Then I have "composed" the following prescription for Karl himself, as the doctors say!

Numero uno, daily caning, and indeed of all those who push, strike, and josh Karl, exclude him from play, or gift him something. He receives one sandwich from me.

After that, Karl receives for four weeks the administration of the most minor post of honour, namely the uplifting of paper, bread, fruit remains, and the like in the schoolroom. After four weeks, he advances to filler of the ink pots.

These means are to start with of no use at all. An effect will only then show when Karl, as I certainly hope, becomes angry at me because he thinks the preferment of the post is mockery. Then his soul will be beginning to react, it is reacting to mockery. How happy I will be over this quiet bristling. I want to take advantage of it, do not want by any means to suppress it by great friendliness.

By and by, Karl will feel that I am favouring him. Then his mood will suddenly change, and the second, better reaction will occur — the secret joy over his receiving preference. I also do not suspect now that he will ply his business especially eagerly, that he will only when the next higher stage is climbed, when namely the desire arises to receive preference. With that personal striving begins.

I will, when this desire is clearly active, again allow an advancement to occur; Karl will distribute the exercise books. That is already a quite high office, and if we have only got so far, it is very good, even if yet no great self-confidence will be present because of the position's subservient character. But, I know that from this moment on, Karl will not be despised by his fellow students anymore. From then on, it will progress quicker.

The next stage will be the most wholesome. I will instruct Karl to fetch me a glass of water, and drink this water before the other children. That will be somewhat difficult for me personally, since I am very easily seized by revulsion, but I will drink the water, and indeed a glass every day from Karl's hands. That will rehabilitate him, and I am convinced that this wholesome stage will be a spur for him to emancipate himself, at least as respects face and hands, from dirtiness. Even with his grandmother! But when that is first achieved, then Karl will have adduced the proof of his own awoken strength of will, and then I will say my "gratias", for Karl will have been saved.

There remains then still the hard work of freeing him from his grandmother. I do not want to have him fetched into the orphanage. From egotism! He is for me too interesting a student. But he must get away from his grandmother.

A circumstance is of use to me. The pond builder is terribly afraid of death, and bears the greatest fear with every storm. On that I am building my somewhat adventurous, but hopefully expedient plan. The pond builder does not like encountering me, and does not like seeing me. Once he said to me, "You always look at someone as if they have stolen something from you. Anyone could be afraid of your eyes."

That is quite good. Dear God will someday send a quite powerful storm. Then I want to seek out the pond builder, and talk with him.

But should he remain hard, well, then I can also end up using the boy, that is, I cannot use him at all, but with an annual income of 900 marks, all sorts of things can be arranged.

\*\*\*

Poor children! I have only three of them, and yet I would like to hesitate sometimes, because I do not think I am equal to the task.

With pain and yet also with poignant respect, I think of you, you courageous battlers who have a worse struggle than I in my wholesome little village. I see you standing, surrounded by the muck of depravation and battling the worm which eats at the tree of humanity, which gnaws at the roots, and drills into the trunk, and which also thrusts its poison fangs to the tender shoots. Oh, brothers, you have the poorest of all the poor children — those tempted by vice early and often! Oh do not let yourselves be scared by the poisonous breath of the atmosphere which blasts at you when you go to confer the sacred gift of your assistance to the poor. Put aside all disgust, disgust is a weakness; yes, let yourself be hated, mocked, misjudged, rewarded with ingratitude, but just do not become weary! I know well — anyone who wants to recognise the insignificance of his power places himself in such a struggle; I know that our weapons — prayer, instruction, admonition, requests, threats, punishment — fail most often precisely on the mired battlefield of the deepest social misery; but I know also that nothing must remain untried, that some have yet been victorious, even when everything seemed lost.

Think of the crown, you dear battlers! — —

# FATE
## (TWO SHORT TALES)

## I. Marooned

"**... Y**ou are suffering when all is said and done from nicotine poisoning", the professor and specialist in heart complaints concluded his diagnosis. "Are you a heavy smoker?"

The patient nodded.

"Yes, my dear man, that is your gravedigger. Your heart function is so disturbed that —"

"Professor, smoking is my only enjoyment", the patient objected.

"No use! If you do not break it off completely, you will be a dead man a year from now."

The patient sighed, and the Professor wrote out a prescription.

"So, call on me again please. That's 10 marks! Where do you live then, Mr Herter?"

"In ...n!"

"Where is that?"

"By X!"

Paul Keller

"And where is that?"

"On the Russian border!"

"Lord, such a region! And you are a teacher?"

"Yes, Professor."

"Hm, hm. Let's say 8 marks then."

"Please, Professor, here's 10 marks."

"As you will! Adieu!"

On the street, Herter stood deep in thought in the middle of the road. He paid no attention at all to the vehicle traffic.

"Hey! Hey! Won't you step aside, man!"

He was able to directly spring to the side and heard still how the coachman cursed the "stupid farmers"; then he was already getting into danger again from an electric car swishing past. The public laughed, and Herter hastened away quickly until he turned into a quiet side street.

He stopped before a "show window". It certainly only exhibited a few eggs and little pieces of cheese; but he did not see it at all. He was merely thinking all the time of how the Professor had forbidden him from smoking. Then a class comrade occurred to him who had been employed here in the big city.

"Do you know perhaps where the teacher Müller lives?", he asked a passerby.

"Müller?", the person being addressed laughed. "I know about four or five dozen people with that rare name, but there is not a teacher among them. Try looking it up in the address book."

"Address book! Where?"

"Well everywhere; for example, in the cigar shop over there. You are surely a little bit new from the countryside, aren't you?"

Herter turned dark-red.

"Excuse me; I was so lost in thought." —

In the cigar shop, he learnt the desired address from the address book.

"What else would you like?", the shop assistant then asked.

Herter looked at him wide-eyed.

"Yes, for the sake of the address book. alone — you will buy something though?"

"But I must not smoke at all."

"The devil, why did you come into a cigar shop then? This isn't an information bureau."

Herter was in deathly embarrassment.

"Please — then — one dozen —."

And he shoved the cigars in his breast pocket.

How wistfully he stepped back into the street. At first he thought of nothing at all, then Müller occurred to him again.

Had had fabulous luck, the fellow. He had not been a great light of the church in the seminary; he had copied the essays and mathematical exercises completely off Herter in touching faith. But had come to the big city. And then his marriage! His wife was thought to have furnished him with an enormous wealth. How it just is! Müller is a tall, broad-shouldered man, has cheerful brown eyes and a coal-black moustache, can dance excellently, dispenses over several dozen jokes, anecdotes, and well-mannered sayings picked up somewhere, can be alternately exuberant and sentimental, and has thus all the qualities which pertain to the ideal image of most young ladies.

Two of Müller's utterances occur to the lonely man striding along. "You know, Herter", he said once, "when I have watered down and copied your essay with forced effort ten times, I am always afraid that the seminar teacher will say to me, "Müller, you did not do that alone!" And a second on departure, "Herter, if someday you are a school inspector somewhere, and I the second

71

teacher in a little town in your district, then be a little lenient with me."

That was almost 30 years ago. And now? Müller is now an affluent man, established in the metropolis of the province, and he? In ...n by X on the Russian border, "Lord, in such a region", as the Professor said.

Herter paused by a large shop window with mirrored panes again. He looked almost derisively at his image in the mirror. The hat old, worn and sweaty around the edges, the linen crushed, barely clean, the overcoat threadbare, shabby, far too wide for the gaunt figure. And the face?

The wild beard would be forgettable, also the unattractive lines and angles; but the eyes are dead, nothing lies in them of the sunny look of a fresh intellect, barely a lost spark smoulders under the grey ash. This face has not gleamed warmly for a long time in the radiance of an enthusiastic thought, no deep thought has paled this forehead, no better passion has drawn its marks about this mouth, the physiognomy offers nothing gratifying. The good psychologist would barely infer by his aspect the expired, noble germs of spirit.

The lonely man in the big city slaps his hands before his face as if seized by a sudden agony. Then he staggers onwards, wearily, slowly.

Only late does it occur to him that he wanted to visit his acquaintance. Then he becomes conscious of having already forgotten the address again. That does not distress him though; he would not have gone there.

He knows well that he is free of envy, but at the sight of the unfamiliar happiness, his misfortune would seem too hard to him, and at the thought of the past, of the ideals, the hopes with which his friend and he had gone into life, the mockery of fate would consume his soul completely.

# Fate (Two Short Tales)

Before he intended, he is at the train station. Just then a train is stopping there, and he climbs in. In a corner, he finds space. About him an indescribable mixture of tobacco haze, and the smell of garlic and emanations of Sunday clothes that had not been used in a long time. He knew that, and yet it barely disgusted him. A sad sign!

The carriage wheels run and rattle monotonously on the rails; Herter sits in his corner of the carriage, and thinks of himself. A picture occurs to him of an army commander who went out to conquer the entire world, and became marooned by shipwreck on a lonely island. There he pined away, not so much from physical hunger and thirst as from unquenched desire for great deeds. He thinks he is like the poor shipwrecked man.

What hopes he entertained, and how many of them he also really could not fulfil! There, a foolish, impulsive, immature remark of a political nature, and he wandered in exile forever. How he has atoned too for his error, what he has also done to escape the ostracism — in vain.

Then he wanted to lend his dreary position an idealistic light, he talked himself with ardent effort into believing he wanted to be a pioneer for culture at the last and most difficult posts, but when he succumbed to the ingratitude and crudity, he threw aside at the time forever, laughing bitterly, the highest good of his heart, his idealism.

When he then took a wife, their souls did not speak to each other. His body yearned for something dear, for a little care. The wife worsened his calamity. She gave him children, they died. Barely for his anguish! She showed no trace of understanding for his intellectual needs, she did not raise him intellectually, but drew him down into stupidity.

His joyless, peaceless home! He was horrified when he thought of it.

He had had a single delight up to now — smoking. There you did not need a second person for it, not the unenjoyable company of the village tavern, not the incurious wife, nobody. He smoked, smoked until his veins swelled, a nervous excitement befell him, and he finally fell with heated face into a dull dreaming. That was up to then his only enjoyment.

And now?

"If you do not break it off completely, you will be a dead man a year from now", the Professor had said.

Herter stares before himself. A dead man! Would that not be salvation?

It suddenly occurs to him that he has forgotten to hand over the Professor's prescription to a pharmacist. At his home, however, there is no pharmacy for miles. Again he ponders. Does he want to become healthy? Must he? Can someone ask that he deny himself the only delight gruesome fate has left to him, just to fritter away such a joyless, pointless life?

He grasped convulsively with his hand for his chest. A quiet, seductive crackling. The cigars!

Herter starts to tremble, a dark redness rises in his face, all the fibres of his body long for the accustomed enjoyment.

There — a grasp for the pocket, the lighting of a match — Herter smokes.

The whiff rushes in racing haste as if it could not drive the unfortunate man quickly enough back to the place where he lost his ideals, his happiness, and his strength.

But he sits and smokes and smokes. And a year from now? — —

# II. The Philistine

When someone has passed the entrance examination for the seminary, he runs probably with extremely red face and sparkling eyes through the streets of the town, jostles someone here, sets off there with a bold leap over the gutter, goes for a change ten steps at a gallop, shouts at all acquaintances who encounter him, in a curt, self-confident style of the victory telegram, a few disjointed remarks over the fortunately passed exam, and reveals by his entire bearing the size of his feeling of happiness.

When the same person has later happily dealt with the rectory examination, he goes home somewhat more calmly. He has become older, the ebullient sanguinity of early youth has gone up in smoke. But success is also now still the waker of joy. The black-clothed figure instinctively stretches a little taller, a fine red covers the cheeks, a peculiar gleam lies in the eyes, and the gait is also quicker and more elastic than usual.

Exactly so did someone come out of the examination hall years ago. He was a handsome, tall man, and may have already passed thirty. Acquaintances did not meet him in the street; he was a stranger to the place. Thus he also did not find the nearest way to the post office after which he was striving.

On the way, he mulled over his life. He had already been a quite quiet fellow as a child. His father had died prematurely, and his death had made his mother into a quiet woman. She loved only her grief and her love, and her son shared both loyally. They also shared the sorrows of the years of study, for it was difficult for both, for him the learning, and for her the maintaining of a livelihood. But because they were both loyal, the blessing was forthcoming.

Model students will always delight more in the recognition of their teacher than the sympathies of their fellow students, and Ernst had, as respects his conduct, always been a model student. While his comrades went for walks, "found a piece" in distant village taverns with students' importance, or shook off the ash of their cigars with the air of connoisseurs in the grass of secluded field margins, Ernst sat at home with his mother. He was never "entirely finished", but chatted with his mother, consulted with her over the small budget, and held the wool for the knitting of the next socks.

His mother was always so touched over her son. But Ernst did not "impress" his comrades, and one who stood in especial eminence, because he had learnt from a related student the "salamander rubbing"*, chided him once for being a "philistine". He remained the "philistine", and Ernst was so docile in nature that this name remarkably did not annoy him.

Later in office, he remained loyal to his way of life. His mother lived with him, and she also formed almost his only contact. He avoided beer drinking and cigar smoking completely. His colleagues called him only a "funny bird", then a "scrooge", and when it was seen by and by that he was wronged by these descriptions, someone thought they had fallen on the right one and said, "He is simply a philistine".

With that he was thus quite discounted socially, and he could hardly complain over it. The young ladies mostly made fun of him after they had thoroughly annoyed themselves long enough over the "dried cod". He

---

\* [Translator's note: this was a student ritual: all participants stood, and drank on the command "ad exercitum salamandri", called "Prost!" (i.e. cheers), then either rubbed or clinked their glasses simultaneously on the table.]

endured that with manly dignity. He became more attentive when an influential person of the town in which he held office said to him, "The Rector will with his great age hardly remain in office for much longer. You are ready for the exam, and will certainly pass it. You are treasured for the sake of your zeal; you would certainly be worth considering with an allocation of the rectorship. Only you must be somewhat more sociable, don't take my well-meant advice wrongly. Such a thing is desired of a man in a leading position. So get married finally!"

At that Ernst turned a fiery red. He got the shivers when he thought of young ladies, and would have been unable to flatter any of them for all the world.

Excepting — one.

She was also such a quiet soul. He had only seen her a few times. But once she had squeezed his hand, gazed at him with a moist look, and said, "You are so good to your mother!" Since then he had been in love with her. If he could only have told her! They could now have been happy together, his mother, her, and him. But he cannot say it to her; he is indeed a philistine. The name goes through him like a stab to the heart. Then it comes like sudden courage over him, a resolve rises up in him, and his head lifts higher, and his feet hurry more quickly. He wants to be bold, wants to show by telegram not only his mother, but also her the fortunate discharge of the exam. Whether it might or might not be proper, she should read from the short message his love.

At the post office, he meets several examination comrades, also his classmate Fritz from the seminary. He is just then writing his twelfth postcard. How jolly he is, always jolly, and yet already has five little children at home. Would that anyone had a small part of his happy temperament!

Before the despatch forms which hang on the wall, Ernst pauses indecisively. Then he tears with a quick grasp two forms from the wall. The despatch to his mother is soon formulated. But the other! He ponders, ponders, and then he writes. When he reads it though, he turns dark-red, a nervous trembling runs over his body, and then — he slowly tears the despatch in two through the middle. — —

He hands over the telegram to his mother, then he berates himself full of impotent fury. Before him stands Fritz, his classmate. Only he does not hear at all what he says to him; then it becomes clear to him. He should come that evening for a few beers together.

"Ah, you know, Fritz", he stutters, "I cannot tolerate beer — you know, my constitution, and then tomorrow quite early —".

"Rubbish! I admit that you were a true monster of solidity in the seminary, you know, you were our phil-istine. But to exclude you today from a little festive nip —".

"I will come! When does it kick off!"

"At eight o'clock. I'm pleased! Until then!"

They part. Ernst walks thoughtfully to his dosshouse out in the suburbs. He is depressed, deeply discontented with himself. But it shall be different, he wants to pull himself together, for her sake.

On the bridge over the river which he must pass over, he pauses for a while, and gazes at the busy bust-ling of the boatmen. He diverts himself thereby, and comes into a better mood. —

Promptly, as is his way, he steps into the specified local on the strike of eight that evening. There is nobody there yet, he is the first. That amazes him. Only towards ten o'clock is everyone gathered.

The mood, however, is animated from the beginning. The exam with its hundreds of contingencies is gone through once more. Jokes are made, everyone is in the best of moods. Ernst too is very excited, and takes a lively part in the conversation. He has even been talked into smoking a cigar. The beer is certainly not to his taste, although the others praise it inordinately. But they make toasts, clink glasses, and they drink together.

Already after the second glass, he is becoming quite strange. Since they are, however, in this way celebrating the teaching profession, he wants in no way to stand back. And he ordered a third glass. With much effort, he drinks it slowly, then he wants to go. But then a lively protest rises from all sides, and his classmate Fritz calls out, "Eh, it would be still more beautiful to run away now when it just getting cosy. Unfortunately, you have no wife to whose health we can toast, not even an official fiancee. But a secret love — — magnificent, see though how he turns red, like a teenager! Cheers, cheers to Ernst's secret love!"

Bright laughter, still brighter clinking of glasses; but Ernst grasps a full glass, and drinks and drinks until his eyes almost stream from his head and — until the glass is empty.

"Bravo, bravo!", the others clap applause; but Ernst throws a taler on the table, "There Fritz, pay for me! Adieu!"

And he is outside. The night is so humid, so humid. With slow, shuffling steps, Ernst goes down the street. He comes to the bridge over the river. A lightning bolt blazes across the dark sky, the black waves on the river whisper quietly. All at once, the strength abandons Ernst; a trembling befalls his body, sweat surges from his pores. Then he feels ill, a strong nausea befalls him. He helplessly looks around, then, a retching — he bends over the low iron railing of the bridge.

Paul Keller

Suddenly a cry, "Merciful God!", a splashing into the water! — — — The next morning, the eel fishermen found him.

# THE OLD AND THE NEW SCHOOL CUPBOARD

There was once a very aged school cupboard. Age had afflicted it badly. Even two or three years ago, people were saying, "It looks quite good for its years", but that was the pitying flattery that you use so often with the old, nothing more. The school cupboard felt quite well itself that it was not much use anymore; its legs were rotten and rickety; in its headboard, two ugly joints gaped just like a pair of menacing furrows, and there had been rips in its back for years.

"Age brings it about in me thus", the school cupboard thought to itself very stalwartly, but did its duty faithfully day after day despite its frailty. And even if a little dust sometimes fell through its poorly closing doors onto the students books, it caused no significant damage.

But yesterday the new teacher, who had only been two or three months in the place, had come into the schoolroom, had cleaned his pince-nez, then examined the cupboard with sharp eyes, and finally said with less benevolent voice, "A rotten piece of furniture! Just as well that tomorrow the new school cupboard comes! Then you will head to the woodshed, old fellow!"

Then something had cracked in the old cupboard. Had it been a man, then you would perhaps have said that its heart had broken. —

The old cupboard had leant in its corner the entire night almost out of its mind; but since day had broken, it was suffering the most terrible torture which there is ... fear. When the doors opened in the living room of the teacher, it started, and when a wagon came rumbling along, it trembled in all its joints.

"They are bringing the new one", it thought. When the door opened, and the teacher entered with the cabinet makers, the old cupboard threatened to lose its mind in its agitation, but it listened to everything the men said.

"Shall we take the old cupboard out now, teacher?"

"No, it may remain here until tomorrow. There are all sorts of things in it which I could not easily clear out yet, I do not have time for it now either. Just place the new cupboard for the time being next to the old; there is room there."

That the cabinet makers then did too, and then they went. The teacher sat down at his desk, and turned to a pile of books and the red ink. The old school cupboard, however, sighed deeply. A postponement!

To examine fifty student essays which all bear the title 'The Camel' does not belong to the great pleasures of life. The teacher reads, dips into the ink, writes, strikes out, sighs, and taps his foot from time to time. Many teachers act similarly in making corrections. This one might in addition not be all too richly blessed with the virtue of patience; he is so provoked over one essay that all his fingers twitch to set below it the censure 'See the title!"; but he masters himself, and just throws the pen away. Despondent, he props his head in both hands.

# The Old and the New School Cupboard

"What an enormous work, creating order in such a school!"

It was very warm in the room, the teacher had given many lessons today, in short, his eyes closed over all his fury and his despondency, and his head sank down onto the desktop, gently, gently ...

The old school cupboard squinted with its only eye, which it had in the manner of bird houses in its head board, at the slumbering teacher, and then to the side at the new cupboard ...

The new one was very tall, very wide and very yellow.

"Whether it will greet me?", the old one thought. "It is younger than me, and I was here before it."

But the new one did not stir. Then finally the old one could not bear it any longer.

"Colleague!", it said very quietly and very modestly.

No answer.

"Dear colleague!"

"Well?"

"You will be my successor, won't you?"

"Admittedly, a successor is in any case also very much needed."

That was now seriously uncharitable of the new one, the old one also felt it as a painful stab; but it composed itself.

"Colleague", it said, "every man becomes old and also every cupboard. Is that a disgrace?"

"A disgrace — hm — no!"

"And will you not also become old?"

"O—ld? M—e? Oh, I am of a strong constitution. But — admittedly — hm — hm — — ah — yes!"

"Age is something very bitter, colleague!"

"Something bitter! Eh, how so? You serve out your time, become old, and step down. That is all."

"That is all! Alright! But the 'stepping down' is not at all so easy, dear colleague."

"That I don't understand. Anyone who is old is also weary, and anyone who is weary needs rest. The world, however, demands fresh strength!"

"And yet I stick to my claim. If you put yourself in my position, you would now be made leftover — leftover — colleague — leftover!"

"Hm, that would be terrible admittedly! But then that is something else, I am young, in love with work, I cannot be leftover."

"Nobody wants to be leftover, colleague, nobody, the old no more than the young. We all believe in our strength; this belief keeps us erect. When we start doubting it, the anxious hours come to us, and someone comes who denies our belief in ourselves or even laughs at it, he cannot hurt us more than by that. Oh, there is something peculiar about us — cupboards! And exactly the best of us like least of all to become old."

The new one fell silent for a little while, then it said, "That sounds right! From where do you know all that?"

"From where do I know it? Oh, many a book has been placed in me with which I was able to hold a secret dialogue. From the books, I have learnt much, but more instructive was what I experienced."

A small pause occurred. Then the new one said, "Old sir, you could actually tell me something. It cannot hurt one as a newcomer if you are given a little orientation, and then it is also quite boring here. The man there is sleeping, and the fire is burning less actively. In the workshop from which I came, it was more cheerful. Particularly when glue was being cooked up!"

"Ah, the workshop, right, colleague", the old one was aroused, "there are no more beautiful memories than those. Indeed you sometimes did not feel quite right when you were planed and polished by someone, for you marveled at how smooth you already were. But it was necessary, very necessary, and when the frames of a

84

cupboard do not want to close properly, there is nothing better than to have the chisel thoroughly help. Otherwise the cupboard remains its life long a pitiful thing, it gapes and yawns to all ends, and it falls apart prematurely. And it was beautiful, very beautiful!

I think still with a hearty delight of the conversations which we unfinished cupboards had with one another when the master had closed the workshop for the evening. There one dreamt of gold and silver which it would have one day to keep safe, a second of juicy pieces of meat and honeycomb which would be locked away in it, a third wanted to become a very famous cupboard which contained thousands of books with a hundred thousand pieces of wisdom, etc. Was that not very droll of us future school cupboards?"

"Extraordinarily droll! But with us it was also so."

"It may be thus everywhere, and it is nothing bad, but something quite natural; later each notes early enough of itself that it is neither a case for jewels, nor a larder cupboard, nor a bookcase for a professor's room, but a school cupboard."

"How did it go for you later, old sir?"

"I made my entrance into the schoolroom at the same time as a young teacher."

"Was that a long time ago?"

"A very long time ago! It was about the time when the little lock had not yet been invented for the school cupboards, and nor the so-called regulations for the schoolteacher. Do you know what the regulations are?"

"No."

"It is no matter either! Let me continue simply. The young teacher stood happily beaming before me, and said, "A very beautiful cupboard!" You will not find that immodest of me, colleague, he really said so. I was at the time a nice brown on the outside and a nice white on the inside, and did not have many snags."

"I'm convinced, old sir!"

"We thus began together, the young teacher — and I. My master was not rich. He brought a small pile of books which was not very large, and locked them in me. That was too few for me, and he may have noticed my chagrin. There he said, 'Do not be irked, dear cupboard! I know well that you cupboards appraise the books by the quantity and the bindings, you do it like so many men who also think woodenly like you; but I will not buy more books than I can pay for and study in-depth. So that you are compensated now, however, I want to elevate you to my money safe.'

I confess, colleague, that I was very proud at this moment. But I was terribly disappointed. He brought a small box which was only as large as his palm, and which smelt of chemist's pills which it probably also contained previously.

'Here, dear cupboard, that is my money box! Though it isn't entirely full, there is merely a quarter of a year's income in silver in it; but keep the treasure safe!'

So the 'box' was not once entirely full! And the few talers were meant to last for an entire quarter! Oh, they were sad times, colleague! How often my good master leant on me in the evenings, and consumed a slice of buttered bread which really did not carry the right to that name; how often he gazed sighing into the pill box which had always long since been empty when the end of the quarter still lay far off. But I creaked my door, partly out of fury over the fate of my master, but partly also because my hinges had not been greased. Dear God, grease was expensive!

It was always the most cheerful and lively in the early mornings when the children came to school. There everybody was jumbled up, little boys and girls, younger and older, nice and naughty. Their total was always recorded with chalk on my left side — over 150! There a school cupboard has nothing to laugh about, colleague! Even if you stand there so taut and imposing, one will dare to scratch your polish sometime, and another to storm in fury against your doors. If you do not stand quite fast there, the black ink runs over inside, and an ugly stain is made on the pure white of the interior.

And just my poor, good master! Ah, colleague, how he worked! Oh, he knew how to tame the wild mob, and almost never took out the hazel rod which lay locked in me. He commanded the children with his look, with his words. Often, when he spoke of God in heaven, it was so still in the class that you could have heard how the woodworm was boring in the ceiling. And he knew how to talk about nature so sweetly, so enthrallingly that once, when he was talking about the tall green firs by the forested lakes in the mountains, I had to think about my youth, deeply shaken, and a drop of sap poured from my wood like a tear.

And he never rested. He went from one to the other, he was kind to and fond of all of them, and all hung on him with childish trust. Often I noted how he was tired, felt how he trembled gently when he leant on me for a second; but when he was quite exhausted, he did not come to me, but went to his desk for a little while.

Do you see, colleague, what hangs above the desk on the wall? Humans call it a cross. It is also only made of wood, just like us, but a wonderful power must reside in it — for every time my good master seemed tired to the point of collapsing, or when a child had extremely irked him, or when his teaching could not find solid ground, he looked up there for two seconds, and then — he was calm and as keen as ever.

Then a new time came. Will you just gaze through the window, colleague? The schoolhouse stands high up, and you have a delightful view from here. Do you see the house down there in the valley, behind which the tall lime trees stand? That is the mill. The early moon stands over it, just like it once did, and the rustling of the water sounds gently from there, just like formerly. At the time that my master stood at the window and gazed down, he pressed his hand to his heart, and a red-ness poured over his cheeks and across his forehead. Oh, those were holy, solemn hours, it was so still in the schoolroom that I heard the pounding of my master's heart, and it beat loudly and restively. And once, when it was beating quite fiercely, he pressed both hands before his face, and stepped before the cross. There he stood for a long, long time. The moon threw its silvery light through the window, it fell on the crucified one, and then it was as if the suffering features brightened, and as if they smiled, gently ... graciously.

On another day, my master stormed into the room, excited like I had never seen him. He spread his arms out, seized me stormily with both hands, shook me so that the ink in me tipped over, but not the black, rather the red, and cried, 'School cupboard, dear, loyal friend, I must tell you — she is mine!' —

Then he was already outside again. I must confess, I did not comprehend him, I only guessed that something good had happened. But after a few weeks, all became clear to me — we were getting married.

It is good for our sort when a woman comes into the house, believe me, colleague. For even if someone is a diligent teacher, it cannot also be said that he also un-derstands how to properly treat a cupboard. But the women ... all respect! Hardly in fact was the woman in the house than she was already appearing in the school-room, turning, cleaning, wiping and also taking me in hand. The hinges of my doors were oiled, I was carefully dusted off from top to bottom, all the boards inside were wiped down and then — no, colleague, what now comes was the most beautiful thing in my entire life.

# The Old and the New School Cupboard

Think, she placed on each shelf a beautiful, white paper, and on the edge of each paper, the most delightful points were cut out. Such a splendour, you could barely imagine, colleague! I naturally thought my master would fall into raptures over me, but when he saw me, he merely laughed. I resented him a lot for that, and he was only able to conciliate me over it by squeezing the young woman's hand and saying, 'How cosy and sweetly you are configuring my home!'

Ah, colleague, that was a happy time, and it remained so for a long, long time. My master worked with doubled strength in class, and I was always brightly polished and clean. It went well for both of them. With the young woman, by and by, lovely little children came into the schoolroom, four in all. The little ones sat on the benches, and the eldest placed himself before them and played teacher.

Then I heard once hurried, hastening steps in the schoolhouse. They went up the stairs, down the steps. Anxious, worried words were heard, in which a quiet crying was mixed. Then a fine carriage came rolling along, from which a gentleman climbed who wore gold framed glasses. The gentleman was in the house for an hour, then he went away again. I listened, and was astonished. Then the night came.

Then the door is suddenly torn open, almost at midnight. The master! The moon shines into his face. How he looks! The face pale, eyes hot, his hair tousled. With swaying steps, he gropes his way to the benches before his desk. There he falls to his knees. I can still see how he raised both hands, and can hear his voice, mute, clenched, 'Lord, do not do this to me!'

Even in the same moment, I heard a scream, it echoed shrilly, desperately, wildly through the quiet schoolhouse. It was not him — only a woman screams thus.

After three days, the schoolchildren sang in the school hall, and then I saw three small, white coffins carried from the house ... the three ... youngest ..., colleague, ... in ... one day. It seemed to me as if I died with them.

When my master again stepped into the schoolroom, he had — grey hair; and when I again saw the woman, I would have almost never recognised her. So ill, so pale, so miserable did she look. I feel now still with a shudder how slowly, how wearily her hands glided over me.

A year later, she was dead. — Colleague, you know, ... she ... could not ... get over it.

Again my master came into the schoolroom. This time, he did not sway or sob, but he walked quite, quite slowly. And when he leant wearily on me, it seemed to me as if his heart were not beating anymore.

Then I did not see him for long months, he was very ill. A young man stood in for him. But I believe the children were more with the ill man than the healthy man. They loved their teacher a lot, and prayed for him. The prayer, however, was one he taught them. So it helped — he got well. When he came into the class, he had wrinkles, but he smiled.

And now he was working again, like only a man can work. Sometimes I thought he wanted to overstress himself intentionally. But to my delight, he once said, 'Strict work is the only medicine which can keep me upright.' —

Thus long years passed. I felt my feet turning rotten and my colour paling. And in all the long years, my master stood in his place assiduously, untiring. Every year, a gentleman came, called the 'school inspector'. He always spoke very good words to him, and squeezed his hand warmly.

My master remained quite alone. Only in the holidays did his eldest, his only one, his son, the student, come. How often he counted the days to the next vacation on the calendar which hung on my wall. His only one, his love! —

Then one afternoon, as my master was writing their at the desk, a man with a colourful cap came who brought a small, folded up piece of paper. When my master opened it, he turned white as the wall, a broken slurring came from his mouth, his eyes protruded from their sockets, his hands passed groping in the air, and with a croak, he broke down right next to me.

The next morning, the children told of how the school's Johannes had fought with another student and been killed by him. — —

This time, my master did not get ill, he continued coming to school. But he was no longer recognisable. He spoke slowly, dragging, little. Mostly he sat at his desk and stared at nothing. His eyes had a glassy expression from that day on.

Almost two years passed thus. Then the school inspector came again, but not the old one, rather a new one. He said much, and became very excited, and at the end he said my master must be pensioned off. He became quite pale. I still hear now his plea, 'Not yet! Not yet now! It will get better with me; I must work, and I always liked so much being a teacher.'

But the other man did not want to hear.

Then one day, my master really took leave. What he said to his children, I did not hear; but when he stepped over to me, I came to.

"Farewell, old, loyal comrade", he said quietly, and caressed my door lovingly with his hand. Then he went. But my headboard sprung in that very hour. —

Now the new teacher came. I do not want to vilify him. He is diligent, but no more diligent than my master was before he received the evil note, for that would be impossible. He says many things which my master did not say, but he also leaves out much which was very, very beautiful. He looks at me with disapproving eyes, and I cannot resent him for it, for I am ugly and old. That he wants to have me chopped up, certainly hurts me, but it hurts me much more that he often speaks with such little fondness of my good master. He has grumbled so often over him, and once he even called him to himself an incompetent, neglectful predecessor. He did not know how much my master worked and suffered, he is still young and cannot know what my master once said, 'The teacher's life is not poor in happiness, but infinitely much sorrow also lies in the span of time between taking the oath and the last closing prayer.'" —

The old school cupboard fell silent; but a full drop of sap flowed down from the new one. He was still struggling for words to lend expression to his agitation, when the teacher, who had heard everything in dream, sprang up.

He stood still for a little while, then he seized his head with his hand.

"Oh, how unjust and foolish I was!" And with a leap, he stands before the old school cupboard.

"You shall not be burnt, loyal cupboard, I will ask your old, good master whether he does not have a place for you. I will also give him your regards, for I am going to him soon. I have much to atone for, I must give him good words, the best words I know!"

# THE TRAMP

I had only just been in place a few days as teacher in the village and was of course not yet grounded in the affairs of that village. I did not even know my neighbours, had also hardly any desire to make my efforts around their acquaintance especially hurried. Too many acquaintances is an evil thing. The "good acquaintance" knows you far too exactly, and he is far too much penetrated by the conviction he is "permitted to take a liberty" for him to not give you at some opportunity the uttermost shame. With friendships it is somewhat different, but they are very thinly scattered in the world.

School was out. In the long path which passed through the middle of the school garden, opening at the end into the village street, the schoolchildren were walking, nice and orderly as is proper, in close procession. I stood likewise, nice and orderly as is proper, in the doorway, and gazed after the children. I certainly still had the secondary aim of "looking at the weather" a little, for in the afternoon I wanted to make a first visit to my colleague in the neighbouring village.

As I am still blinking up at the clouds, a terrible screaming arises suddenly among the children; order dissolves; a great part, particularly girls, come running back to the schoolhouse, another mob, the strongest boys at the front, storms to the village street. It is as if a whirlwind has passed among the children. Breathless, in skittish flight, the girls come nearer. "The tramp!", they shriek, and "the tramp!" is jeered down on the village street.

"Who is the tramp? What does he want?", I ask one girl.

"He wants to shake our hands — ugh!", she answers, and "ugh!" sounds in chorus from the others. There is an emotion, an outrage among the girls, as if an owl has appeared in daylight among the songbirds.

Meanwhile, the shouting on the street becomes more serious. I hastily tear the garden gate open and hurry through the garden down to the village street.

A wondrous image! A man stands in the street, the model of a ragged vagabond. The boys have closed a circle around him, fenced him in completely. The vagabond has stretched out a hand, and holds it out to a boy.

"Child, give my your hand", he said in a pleading tone.

The boy, however, a high-spirited little fellow, strikes the old man with his ruler across the fingers. A laughing and jeering of the others rewards him for his heroic deed.

But the vagabond's face twists in pain and fury. His dead eyes come alive for a moment; a sound wrestles itself from his lips, a quite indescribable sound. I shudder at this sound. But the arousal of the old man does not last for long; the fire in his eyes dies out, he looks slack again, smiling disgustingly like all drunkards.

"Give me your hand", he slurs anew, and stretches his hand out to the boys again. He would have again been struck on the fingers by one of them if my cry of displeasure had not scattered the boys. Momentarily they free the besieged man, withdraw some twenty steps, and wait at this distance for what would follow.

The "tramp" stands before me. He holds his cap in his hand almost reverently; white, wildly disheveled hair flashes at me. With a look, I examine him. I come as a result to that uncomfortable disposition which always seizes someone when they are not clear over their own view and own feeling. Interest and disgust struggle in me and merge together.

Deep, black sacks hang from under his dripping eyes, an ice-grey, stubbly beard sprouts wildly on his bluish red cheeks, a trembling runs over his entire body. An alcoholic of the worst sort. In addition, the torn, dirty clothing. I am in horror of the old man. But some interest is mixed into the horror. The hair would be beautiful if it had not gone to seed so badly, and the forehead is high and contrasts in white from the rest of the swollen face.

"You are the teacher?", the old man asked quietly and no longer slurring.

"Yes! What do you want from the children?"

"One should shake my hand; nothing else."

"And why do you desire that?"

"Because — because — it would do me a lot of good. Anyone to whom a child gives their hand is fortunate!"

With the last words, he looks up. I am startled. I once saw a stag die whose look was exactly like that which I saw just then. What is it with the old man?

"I do not understand", I said uncertainly, and grasp in my pocket. "What do you want?" Then he looks at me once more — deeply saddened.

"Nothing!", he says, turns around, and sways down the village street. He is obviously drunk, perhaps not at all right in the head. What am I worried about!

But it is no use, the excellent "what am I worried about" with which men tend so easily to release the uncomfortable pity from their necks which concern for strangers has woken in them. The tramp does not leave my mind anymore. I sit down at the table with thoughts of him, I even dream of him in the short midday siesta which I keep, and as I make my way to my neighbouring colleague, I am really still thinking of the tramp. I get angry with myself, call myself a "sentimentalist", an "all too trusting drip", and the tramp a "drunken fellow", a "greasy vagabond" — it is no use; I think of the tramp.

My neighbouring colleague is a nice man. He comes towards me with friendly assurance, and we are soon acquainted with each other. Since he is an old bachelor, we are alone, and can chat undisturbed.

In the middle of the conversation, the tramp occurs to me. I relate to my colleague the event of the morning.

"Ah — him", my colleague says, "yes, you know, that is a very sad story."

"You know the tramp?"

"Certainly, he begs through all the local places, and always remains in the district."

"What do you think of him?"

"He is a harmless, but otherwise absolutely depraved man. What he begs, he drinks away with the cheapest booze. He is dirty in a truly disgusting way, the vermin almost feed on him. People stretch a piece of bread or a pfennig out the door to him, just to be rid of him quickly again; but the children hate him. Most flee from him, a few chase him. I myself protect him from the stone throwing of the boys."

"And how do you explain this fear or hate from the children?"

"You used the image of the owl and the songbirds before. It is conspicuously accurate. If the little bird, who pounces fiercely in bright daylight on the predator blinded by the light, has not experienced any harm from this one itself, yet its unfortunate brothers and sisters have suffered under its claws; it feels that instinctively, and hates just as instinctively the spoiler of its race. It is quite similar with the tramp. To the children who vilify him, striking, throwing, he has done no evil. I have never heard of him striking a child; he instead offers each his right hand amicably with the constant plea, becoming part of his manner, "Child, give me your hand". And nevertheless, the children hate him, instinctively, like the forest birds hate the owl. — — The tramp was formerly a teacher. — Because of a sexual crime, he went to jail for years, and then he went the way which so many prisoners do, he became a 'tramp'."

"Terrible! Horrific! When did that happen?"

"It was 25 years ago. At the time, I had just arrived in the district as a very young teacher. They were sad times. Two such cases occurred right after each other. First the teacher of my village went to prison, where he died, and four months later, the teacher of your village, Werner, the 'tramp'."

"Was Werner employed in my village? And that is the tramp?"

"Yes! It concerned at the time three almost fourteen year old schoolgirls. One still lives, and is now the richest property owner of your village. The others both died strangely a year after their marriages from childbirth."

"Very strange!"

"That was a terrible event. When the first of the two young women died, I was at the funeral. We colleagues supported each other at such occasions mutually. Now I still shudder when I think of the funeral. The coffin stands over the open grave, the clergyman speaks the prayer. Then suddenly, as if emerged up from the earth, the tramp stood next to him.

"Save your words, priest", he shouted; "here I want to speak the blessing!"

A kick met the coffin so that it swayed.

"Go to hell, godless, crazy woman! God made your own child strangle you at birth for the sake of the crime which you committed against me. Go to hell — perjurer!"

It lay like a leaden, paralysing shock over the funeral gathering. Nobody stirred; the tramp just slowly left the churchyard.

He received two years in prison for his gruesome oath by the grave.

While he served his time, the second of his former accusers died, likewise giving birth to her first child. When the tramp had served his sentence and learnt of the death of this second, he is supposed to have knelt in the middle of the tavern and thanked God with upraised hands. Then he went to the churchyard, laid waste to the grave mound, and then had to go to prison again for this new gruesome deed."

"And despite all that, you do not doubt at all the guilt of Werner?"

"No! At the trial, he admittedly did not confess, even now he confesses nothing. Only when the schnaps loosens his tongue does he betray himself."

"What sort of man was Werner before?"

"An extraordinarily capable teacher. At the seminary, he was top of his class, our teachers' association chose him despite his youth to be chairman because of his efficiency and eloquence, his school stood with the best reputation."

"Was he not married?"

"No, but engaged. His fiancee was the wife of another when he came out of prison."

A pause occurs. Anyone who looks into an abyss does not say many words; the shudder which seizes him in the face of the black depths closes his mouth.

Black, unholy abyss in the teacher's heart, should I be more horrified by your musty depths, or should my heart hurt with the thought of the abundantly sweet, hopeful happiness which has perished in you? Should I agree in the "Anathema sit!" which human society has repeated in judgement over the unfortunate man, or should I be satisfied with his being outcast, despised, branded, mocked, chased creeping from house to house to fritter away with reluctantly offered breadcrumbs that existence of his which is being consumed by inner and outer vermin? Curse or pity? I think — pity! The guilt is certainly horrific. But the atonement?

Again he stands before me, and again I hear his request, "Child, give me your hand!" I know well what presses the request out of your heart, poor old man. A teacher's nostalgia has grasped you; an ardent yearning has overcome you for the sweet children's love, for the gratifying children's trust which was once yours; you look pining like a banished man at the paradise whose portal is closed to you because you sinned so badly in it, and you beg in vain as if for a drop of grace to cool your tongue, "Child, give me your hand!"

There you might well grasp the booze bottle, I consider it natural; it is a last, sad consequence. —

I share my thoughts with my colleague, he endorses them. A different conversation does not start flowing after that. It is also becoming quite late. We part.

The moon is standing over the lonely country path which I am striding down. In the twilight, I see a cross by the edge of the path. I step closer, and take off my hat. I want to say a Lord's prayer for — the tramp. Then — next to the cross, his white head leaning on the upright, the tramp himself is sitting. We gaze in each other's eyes mutely for a while. Then I begin, "You will spend the night here?"

"Yes, I cannot pay for accommodation today."

"And why do you set yourself right here? Do you have faith in the cross?"

"I have faith in him! He has let me become unhappy, very unhappy, sir, but he avenges me too. Right, you up there, you are avenging me?"

And he looks up at the image of Christ. I shudder. I cannot look at the old man any longer. A ten mark piece flashes in the moonlight, the pocket money for this month. I offer it to him.

"Take it! You can get clean clothes with it from a trader."

Then the old man cries out so that it echoes loudly through the night, "Sir — sir — 10 marks — yes — yes — that is so. Sir, you believe in my innocence?"

And he tears the money from my hand, and presses his lips to it as if insane. But I shake my head sadly.

"Of your innocence, I cannot believe unfortunately, but I have a hearty sympathy for you."

Then it is as if the countenance of the old man turns to stone.

"Take your money back, I don't like it; you give too little. I have received sympathy here and again, but no faith or trust for 25 years. There no clean clothes are any use, sir; the sooner the lice eat you, the better."

And he disappears despite my shouts.

Weeks have passed since then. The autumn has drawn into the countryside with its dreary, melancholic misty days. I have not seen the tramp anymore; but I have thought of him a lot.

The scene at the path-side cross shook me deeply. Again and again the question arose for me of whether he could not be innocent. But he shall surely have confessed his crime for the twentieth time in the tavern. Certainly he was also then almost always drunk. And why this proud refusal to take my gift? Is he so corrupted that he affects a comedy with me to convince me of his innocence, on the assumption I would then support him amply and regularly? No, and if it were all lies, one thing was certain, the terrible look which he threw at the cross, and his plea for vengeance. No man can lie like that. — —

It is almost four o'clock in the afternoon. The November sun struggles with thick mist; it is becoming dark very early today. But I must still take a walk; I have worked the entire day, and my head is humming.

The village street is empty as always. It lies infinitely desolate and melancholy before me; unmoving bare trees stare into the thick autumn mist, dead scrub sways on the edge of the brook. I shiver a little, and I envelop myself tighter in my coat. I am thinking barely of anything, nothing at least of which I am sensible. But as I arrive before Lindenbauer's farmstead, I pause for a little while.

Lindenbauer certainly has the nicest farm in the entire district. This residence is not stately! It looks not at all rustic, it has tall windows and even a balcony. The work buildings are exemplary; on Tuesday there was an agricultural association there to view them. Lindenbauer is in addition the creditor of almost all the middling and smaller property owners of the village. Our sort cannot imagine at all how it might be when you have so much money, when you need never ask, "Is this or that also too expensive for you?"

Onward, schoolmaster, onward!

Mrs Lindenbauer — she is also one of the former accusers of the tramp, the only one who still lives. And how does she live? In abundance, in fortune! What does she even lack? She never has a wish in vain, she radiates health, has a rich husband who lets himself be governed by her, and a child who is certainly the most beautiful girl in the district, Friedel. The old man under the cross must have lied, it would not be possible otherwise for Mrs Lindenbauer to be so happy.

Friedel certainly — she is beautiful, very beautiful, but she has a sensual air to her face. I understand physiognomies. — But calm down, do not be a knocker, go your way.

At the end of the village, I turn around. I indeed wanted to go as far as the cross, because the tramp will not leave my mind at all once again today, but the evening is too dreary and melancholy.

I approach the Lindenbauer's again.

The village street seems uncannily deserted to me right now. My mood is so depressed. Now I am by the picket fence which encloses the Lindenbauer's garden. There is not the slightest breath of wind.

Suddenly something rustles in the scraggly foliage. A woman is walking through the garden. In the twilight, I recognise Mrs Lindenbauer. She is walking quickly, hastily, as if searching for something. Suddenly she pauses. She stands for a second as if rooted to the spot, then a sob, a groan struggles spasmodically from her chest; — now she tosses her arms up in the air, and a shrill note of horror howls desperately through the pale twilight, "Jesus! — Jesus!"

With one leap, I am over the fence. — — — — On the lowest branch of the apple tree hangs Friedel, Mrs Lindenbauer's only child. — — —

I cut Friedel down. Rescue attempts here would be completely in vain, I see. So I kneel down next to the dead girl in the short, bare autumn grass, and pray confused stuff. Next to me, Mrs Lindenbauer cowers.

Her eyes adhere rigidly to the features of the dead girl.

"Hey," she then begins, quietly, in a whispered tone, "do you know why she did it? The shame, schoolmaster, the shame!"

It runs cold over my limbs. So that's why! I am incapable of stirring. Then suddenly the farmer's wife laughs to herself, "Hahaha! Hung yourself have you? Think, what use is it? It'll come out! Hahaha! Wait, the father!"

Great God, Mrs Lindenbauer has lost her mind for shock and pain! — Now a twitch goes through her body; she stands up. She leans on the tree in the dim evening light. The head of her dead child lies at her feet. It seems to me as if my heart had stopped, as if I were also a dead man under this dead person. Mrs Lindenbauer has closed her eyes, a tired twitch plays about her mouth. Then she begins talking in a monotone, "Teacher, I am besides myself! Are you listening? I want to betray something to you. The — tramp — is innocent! All three of us lied at the time. The tramp often punished us so hard when he was teacher. We wanted to get revenge. We knew that a teacher who does such a thing goes to prison. It had happened in the neighbouring village. That is how we knew." —

A cry of horror, of deathly hate towards the terrible woman comes from my mouth. It comes from my teacher's heart, and it concerns the unfortunate brother who was destroyed. Then my look falls on the dead girl, and I am still. Mrs Lindenbauer stands motionless, her look directed rigidly at the blond head of her child. A late leaf falls from the tree, you can hear it falling. Then the farmer's wife begins talking again, "There is one above, schoolmaster, do you believe in him? I have always been frightened of him, but he has done nothing to me. Just my child has hung herself, just my child!"

And she falls down in a faint.

I haul myself mechanically to the homestead. I still hear screeching, screaming voices, then my senses lapse. — Black! —

Friedel is buried. She was interred just as the school-maid was tolling the evening bell. I saw none of that, I am too ill.

Mrs Lindenbauer is in the madhouse. — Incurable! — I think of the tramp as he spoke under the cross, "Right, you up there, you are avenging me!"

Tramp, you made a gruesome prayer; but heaven must have said "amen" to your prayer, because you were such a poor, passed over, downtrodden, innocent, praying man. —

I do not know who told him first. He emitted a gurgling note like an animal when it escapes its cage after a long torment, then he sank down, and lay unconscious for three days.

I found him thus. When he awoke, he smiled without stop. I told him the government would, after his innocence was proven, probably provide him with a pardon pension. It made hardly any impression on him. What would the pension be to him? He does not need it; he is accustomed to the hunger, thirsting, and freezing. But he has something on his heart.

"Teacher," he says, and his voice is trembling, "I have a request, a very big request. Let — me — just — just once — just a single time — again — into the schoolroom!"

The emotion overcomes me. I squeeze his hand.

"Certainly, certainly, my poor, dear — colleague!"

Then he cheers, and kisses both my hands fiercely. He is almost distraught with happiness because he may go into the schoolroom, and because I have called him "colleague". —

Our school inspector has a good heart, the pastor too. They are both present as I go with Werner hand in hand into the schoolroom.

As the old man steps into the room, he closes his eyes, and a tear drops onto his cheek. What might be flowing away in this tear!

And the schoolchildren cluster about him, and shake his hand. —

# The Tramp

It has turned spring. Werner has spent the winter happily and peacefully in the cosy little room which we furnished for him. I was often with him. He has not gone to the tavern a single time.

Today he is receiving the holy sacrament in the church. Next to his hat on the bench lies a small packet. Little bouquets of wild flowers he picked himself are in it. After mass, he carries them to the grave of both young women, and he places one, because Mrs Linden-bauer is distant, with Friedel in the corner of the churchyard.

Werner made complete peace with God and the world. On the same day, as it became evening, he died. He passed away peacefully in my arms.

By his grave, the schoolchildren and colleagues of the district sung alternately, as is the privilege and custom with a — teacher's funeral.

# MOUNTAIN PEACE

I have always been a quite peculiar mountain travel-
ler. To mention two things, I do not take with me any
binoculars, and I never travel in larger companies. Both
seem superfluous to me, even harmful.

The "beautiful view" appears to many to be the
greatest attraction of the mountains, and they lament
when a treacherous cloud frustrates the hoped-for delight. How foolish!

There is something uncommonly charming, perhaps
also elevating, in all at once receiving a view from a
raised point of the greater part of God's beautiful earth,
and in a finely attuned, receptive soul, that colossal image can leave behind a deep impression; but most
observers stand before the giant canvas of the eternal
master like dull fools before a profound work of art.
They argue over the extremely trivial name of some
peak, they rack their brains over whether the village on
the mountain slope is Neu or Alt-Thalgrund, they focus
their binoculars and overstrain their eyes to spy out of a
distant village at least a church tower or a factory chim-
ney, they call out several times dutifully with all the
pathos at their command, "magnificent!" or "quite
charming!", then write in the inevitable mountain inn
on half a dozen picture postcards just as many bad
rhymes, and start the climb down finally with the loud
or at least secret wish, "If we were only below again."

# Paul Keller

I have constantly regretted these poor drips, but I also avoid them, I do not want to be disturbed by them, to have to be annoyed over them. Thus it comes that I know nothing at all of the most visited places of some ranges; I have been on many a lonely height, however, which is described in no guide, and is not named on any map. I am usually not desirous of human company, but in the mountains I like to be alone because you can only find in the solitude what the heart surges for — — peace, silence without and within. — —

It was long ago. The holidays had arrived and I was getting ready for my journey. Money was tighter than usual this year, and so I once again took Goethe's words of good advice to heart, and steered my steps to the mountains of my native Silesia.

My way led me here and there, I had no plan. If you must direct the entire year according to plans, you like heartily to act without a plan for once. And I found on my way that which I sought, solitude, deep solitude, and the leisure to live entirely according to my nature. I came through little villages in which a tourist was rarely or never to be seen, I dined at the tables of farmers, and found accommodation for the night in the little houses of forest rangers. And I found time to admire the lichen, to stare into the soft shimmer of blossoming heather from weathered boundary stones. On a wind-broken fir tree I dreamt like a sentimental poet, and I teased the squirrels like a totally free boy; I felt deeply shaken on lonely heights by the vicinity of God, and not long after-wards I threw little stones like a playing child down from the heights into the little lake in the valley. I would have peered into all the hollow trees, would have liked to stop the ants chatting in their work, I must have sipped from every little spring, and wanted to spin my-self an imaginative little fairy tale about every lonely tree. It was a happy journey! —

# Mountain Peace

I had stopped for a midday rest in a lonely village, and had then set out. At the end of the village, the path passed into a meadow, and you could see no other path as a continuation but a narrow forest path which was visible on the other side of the meadow. I hesitantly asked a farmer who was raking together hay in the meadow, "Where does the path up there go to, dear man?"

"There? Well, into the bush!"

"Into the bush, alright! But where does it continue on to?"

"Continue? It stays constantly in the bush. Nothing but bush! Afterwards comes the mountain ridge, and last of all the quiet peak."

"The quiet peak? What is that?"

"It's a couple of houses, and Waber's people are there, nothing else! It does not even have a crevice! There is absolutely nothing going on there!"

"It's also not necessary that something is going on," I smiled. "How far it is to the quiet peak?"

"Well, it can be two, three, four hours."

"Thank you! Adieu!" —

The quiet peak! When later I was more familiar with the place, I found that a quite different name was flaunted on the place-name sign; but there was certainly no more fitting description for the little village than that which the mouths of the folk had ascribed to it ... the quiet peak.

A plateau spread out on a mountain, a few hectares in size, covered by meadows, and hemmed in all around by sombre fir forest. On this plateau stood six or seven cottages, covered in shingles, a few close to the edge of the forest, and one in the middle of the open area. That was the quiet peak.

It was already evening when I arrived at the quiet peak. The scattered cottages lay in the twilight. A feeling of the deepest loneliness, even of desolation overcame me, and a light shiver merged with it. I stood still, and was for the moment undecided as to what I should do. Then suddenly a gruff voice sounded next to me, "What do you want here?"

I spun around in shock. A man stood next to me in the attire of a mountain resident. He wore jacket and trousers of grey linen, and on his head a straw hat which was somewhat worn on the rim. On his feet he wore sandals. I saw little of his face, since he was standing against the light, but I was able to reckon his age at perhaps 50 years.

"What do you want here?", he repeated.

"I am a tourist", I answered, somewhat apprehensively.

"I see that, and hence I ask what you want here. This place is not for tourists. You can leave your consumptive lungs, your vices and perversities down in the valley, or only carry them to the mountain places which are already corrupted by your lot. But leave us in peace!"

That was rough, but I contained myself, and replied in a friendly tone, "You are quite right if you do not want your mountain peace disturbed."

"Mountain peace? What do you know of mountain peace?"

"I know a lot about it, for I know it. I have sought it because I was often tired from much work and going without, and from resentment of others and of myself. I have sought it, but not on the mountain paths on which the great crowd walks, but on the quiet peaks like this one here is. And hence I am also here today."

The stranger examined me sharply for a long while. Then he asked, "So you are here?"

I nodded.

"And for that reason?"

I nodded again.

Then he seized me roughly by the shoulder, and said, "Now, we will see! Today it is dark, and there is no other place here to spend the night other than with me in the schoolhouse. March!"

"Ah, you are the teacher here? That is well met; I too am a teacher."

I said that to put myself in the highest possible standing with my new host. But he said roughly, "It's all the same."

And he drew me away to the house which stood in the middle of the plateau.

\*\*\*

My summer journey came on that evening to an un-expected conclusion; for I remained for the entire time of my holiday on the quiet peak. I did not get away from the strange man who took me into his house. He shackled me extraordinarily by his strong nature, and when I once really made an air to go on, he rounded hard on me, took my stick from my hand, and did not speak with me for half a day. So I stayed.

And I liked staying. The quiet peak offered me what I sought — intimate, undisturbed interaction with nature, deep silence ... mountain peace. But it offered more. My host, the teacher Stein, was an extraordinarily enigmatic man, and all puzzles have their interesting and instruct-ive aspects, excluding perhaps those which are in the newspapers.

Stein's residence was more than simple. No curtains, no sofa, not even a mirror was to be seen there. The fur-niture, which was also represented by only the most necessary pieces, was mostly unworked or only painted in the most primitive way. You might have thought yourself to be in a hermitage if two things had not con-tradicted it — a valuable, magnificent harmonium which stood in the large main room of the cottage, and a wo-man.

Stein's wife was almost an entire head taller than he was himself, she had a complexion blooming with health, her physique was muscular, almost gigantic, and she looked wondrous enough against the rangy man. At the same time, like most such tall and strong women, she was of somewhat coarse nature, but good hearted. The degree of her intellectual development was very small — Stein talked with her in the same tone as he spoke to the weaver women, and she would not have understood any other language either. She did not com-prehend me most of the time, although I of course avoided all abstract phrases.

I did not have a much higher opinion of the man to begin with. I considered him to be a man who, from low foundations and deficient schooling, isolated from all stimulating intercourse, had fallen victim entirely to rustic ways despite his educational office. Thus it was really only the peculiar charm of the place, not the at-tractions of the persons, which caused me to rest for a day on the quiet peak. But it would soon turn out differ-ently.

With the walk over the mountains which I undertook in the afternoon with my host, I collected plants for study. Stein looked at me uncomprehendingly.

"Have you never sought out plants?", I asked him.

"Oh yes," he nodded animatedly, "but only for the goats."

And he was a teacher! I was quite shocked. I could not prevent myself giving the ignorant man a lecture over collecting plants for study, over the beauty of nature and the usefulness of natural history. He listened attentively, then he asked, "You know surely all the plants?"

"Most of them," I answered, whereby I admittedly turned a little red.

"That must be quite difficult," he noted simply.

"Yes, quite!", I confirmed.

"You know," he continued, "you could actually teach me the names too!"

"All of them?", I asked with amusement.

"Well, not exactly all, but perhaps half."

I was horrified by such simplemindedness. But I took control of myself.

"Well, collect together for my sake the plants whose names you would like to become acquainted with; I will lead the way as far as that towering stone; there I will wait for you. But I will not be able to teach you half of all plant names unfortunately, for that would be a thousand more names than there are hairs on my head."

"Ah, that you say," he acted surprised, then we separated. I was happy that I was rid of him.

After quarter of an hour, he was with me. He had a bunch of plants in his hand.

"Here," he said, "there are 16 sorts."

I was shocked. There were mostly little mountain weeds whose names I did not know. There I had the punishment for my bragging. But I did not want to make a fool of myself.

"Of these plants," I said evasively, "I could only tell you the Latin names, and that would be pointless."

"Oh, I have spoken Latin once before too."

"You? Latin?"

"Yes, I ministrated in the church as a boy."

I looked up quickly. Did this voice not sound like it was mocking? No, such a simple face shows only the genuine simplemindedness. Nevertheless, I found myself in an awkward predicament. I looked through the plants, and of the 16 different examples I knew exactly — three. What to do? There the lying devil was also already at work, "You cannot blame yourself! So tell him some fib; he does not understand anyway, and you can make some fun into the bargain!" And unfortunately, unfortunately I followed the seducer.

"So, if you are absolutely emphatic about it, I will name the 16 plants for you. Pay attention! This little type of moss is called Sequóia gigantea."

"Sequóia gigantea", Stein repeated. "Sequóia is surely small and gigantea types of moss?"

"The reverse!" I said with amusement. The fibbing began to delight me. "But more! That there is a sort of woodruff — Asperula odorata."

"Asperula the wood, odorata the ruff," Stein droned.

"And this prickly thistle is called viola silvestris."

"Viola prickly, silvestris the thistle," the other man memorised.

"This maggoty fungus is called convallaria majalis."

"Aha," Stein exulted, "here it is again reversed, majalis is maggoty and convallaria the fungus."

I would have liked to have laughed aloud! In a cheerful mood, I kept fibbing through all 16 sorts. Finally we were at an end. Stein offered me his hand.

"I thank you. Oh, with you someone can learn something! You must be an enormously clever man! The Latin names are not at all so easy! And if half of them already carry a thousand times more than I have hairs on my head, how much must you have learnt to know most of them, thus almost all!"

I began to be a little ashamed.

"If I might only not forget the words again," Stein continued. "It would be a pity with your effort! I want to repeat everything straightaway please."

I became a little restive. The other man, however, began reciting, "Sequóia gigantea, Asperula odorata, Viola silvestris, Convallaria majalis, Victoria regia", etc. for all 16 names. A dreadful recollection. I turned pale.

But Stein exulted, "Correctly memorised, right? Oh, natural history is a beautiful subject! I want to learn lots with you! And when a stranger comes up here, I want to list everything for him."

"Do not do that," I burst out.

"Eh, why not then? I do not want by any means to act as if everything came from me. The telling of fibs is something shabby, don't you think so too? No, I want to tell everybody that I know all the beautiful names from you, from you who knows thousands more plant names than I have hairs on — —"

"Stop, you should not say that!"

"Why not, you are just too modest! Oh, I will also impress the beautiful words on the schoolchildren! You have yourself said that natural history is beautiful and useful, and the children at least must know what sort of plants grow in your home district."

I was close to despair. If he impressed such nonsense on the children! The children! My conscience was pricked.

"You are so quiet all of a sudden," Stein said.

I struggled for a little while yet; then I cannot endure any longer.

"I — I —", I stammered, "— I — it must be revealed — it is in fact nonsense — all nonsense — that about the plant names, I mean — none are correct — all nonsense — I — I have allowed myself a little fun! Just do not tell — the children!"

Then sheet lightning twitches in the face of the other man. His head colours dark-red, and then — he begins laughing, laughing so ungovernably that the quiet forest echoes from the loud laughter, and I am completely disconcerted. Finally the horrible man begins talking. He chokes out arduously, imitating me, "I — I — it must be revealed — it is — in fact nonsense — utter nonsense — that I believed that — about the plant names, I mean —

utter nonsense — that I would have thought — it would be a right one! I — I — have — also allowed myself a little fun!"

I stood as if touched by lightning. I would have liked most of all to sink into the ground. I had thus hoaxed myself! Oh, this comedian! A feeling of fervent shame blazed through me. I was incapable of looking up. The other man, however, still laughing, gathered up the plants from the ground, and said, "Now pay attention, wise sir! You can learn for your thousands of botanic names these 16 pieces."

And he named the 16 botanic names which I admittedly barely heard. Finally I pulled myself together.

"I must go," I said, "away soon; I have made a fool of myself too terribly! I want to fetch my backpack from your house and then go. Farewell, and don't be cross with me!"

"Oh-oh, it was not meant like that! You have made a fool of yourself, agreed, but you must not run away! It was just a precious joke! You were amused, and I was amused. Why should we be enemies after we have had such a mutual delight? Endure, young man, and repair the harm, that is the right thing!"

It went back and forth for a long time, but finally I stayed.

\*\*\*

Never again did such a powerful reversal occur in my view of a person as with Stein, the teacher from the quiet peak. I learnt to respect, even love this man whom I so strongly underestimated to begin with. If his entire being also remained mysterious to me, yes, often completely incomprehensible, I knew though that he had a noble and clever motive for all that he did. I was in the end incapable anymore of the slightest doubt over him, the man whom I had only known for such a short time.

But you can recognise a strong, noble character, just like diamonds, often from the first single beam which emanates from it, and the bright fire leaves no doubt anymore for the judicious eye.

What seemed most incomprehensible to me with Stein was the disproportionately high sum of knowledge which he united in himself. And yet only two books were found in his household, a bible for him and a prayer book with very large letters for his wife.

Stein himself, however, was a wandering book. Whatever area I might touch on, he showed himself to mostly widely outclass me. Not that he, as in botany, would have made some fun with me. He seemed to have completely forgotten that intermezzo, so painful if also instructive for me.

He did not force his knowledge on me, did not give me magnificent lectures to impress me, instead mostly only a few, aphorism-like remarks which he made when I discussed my views over this or that, but in these curt remarks often a deep wisdom crystallised, substantial enough to make you think about the few words and to study them.

It is explicable that often questions clustered on my tongue over from where he received the great measure of his education, and how it came that such a significant man was placed in the isolated little village.

But I took good care not to express this question, for firstly he would not answer it, and secondly it would have in any case thrown him into a fierce rage.

He loved the lonely people of this little forest village, and he would have considered it a sin against them to deny them even in thought the right to having a competent teacher.

"Oh if I were a genius!", he once said, "yes, if that were not impossible, a genius in all things! Do you know what I would then like most of all?"

I nodded.

"To be schoolmaster on the quiet peak", I said.

He looked at me in surprise.

"Why?"

"The people in the quiet little forest village", I said, "are people as good as the others. They are heirs of equal right to the great estates in all areas of the intellect which wise and noble men of many times and peoples, toiling, brooding, going without, and making sacrifices, worked together on, saved up, and bequeathed to future generations. In the big cities sit many lawyers who share the general genetic make-up; there are thousands of opportunities to enrich yourself intellectually there; all the doors stand open there in the filled storerooms. There it is said, 'Whoever has ears to hear, listens', and 'Whoever has hands to gather, gathers!' Into the remote little villages, however, an isolated messenger is sent to bring the indigent people there their little share of the great, intellectual estate, ... a teacher. When the messenger is a weak man who gathers together little, because he is only capable of carrying a little, or when he is sluggish and does not like to carry much, then the poor little stepchildren in the forest village are in a bad way. By rights, they should choose giants for such messengers, so that even the poorest child in the poorest mountain area would receive their intellectual inheritance."

That was the first time that I saw Stein moved. He squeezed my hand, and said curtly, but warmly, "You are right!" — —

In instruction, Stein almost never let me take part.

"You disturb me and the children," he said; "you could not learn anything by it, and you could give me advice even less, for in the school on the quiet peak, everything is different from down there with you. Why would you want to then?"

There was no schoolroom according to our concept of one. In the teacher's living room, there were two tables pushed together at which the seven students sat with their teacher. But on all the beautiful days the in- struction was held in the open air. I often heard songs ringing out when I was strolling in the nearby forest, and I often saw the mountain schoolteacher standing before his mob in great enthusiasm, and when he raised his hands to the blue sky, when he pointed to the fir trees which hemmed the meadow in earnest silence, when he knelt down with a light flower in the soft grass, and showed it with delighted eye to the children, then I knew that he was speaking of God. — —

A boy had lied to his mother. The entire little village went into an uproar over it which was incomprehensible to me. I questioned Stein. He smiled.

"The sins here are not so everyday as down there in the world. There is little temptation here. For example, when you go through the main sins, you will find that apart from impatience, the fury with work, and a certain degree of intellectual lethargy, the people do not have much outward reason to sin. They are too poor to be haughty, miserly, envious, or immoderate, and their cir- cumstances are too simple and wholesome for them to be able to lust after things.

I can say the life of the individual is nowhere so pub- lic as with us in the hidden mountain forest. That arises from the circumstances being so infinitely simple and transparent. Here no husband can say a loud, furious word to his family without it being heard in all the houses; here no wife can wear a new apron without all the villagers knowing where she took the money from for it; a drunkard would sound bad if he stumbled over this quiet plateau, and the air in the circle of these sombre fir trees is too fresh and pure for you not to soon notice with distaste the seething of a lascivious heart.

All these circumstances contribute to the resulting virtue of the mountain residents, a virtue which is certainly not so deserving of recognition as the confident steadfastness of a struggling soul who remains upright and uncorrupted in the whirl of danger, in struggle and hardship, but also not so deserving as a virtue which is proven in practice.

I would like to say one more thing. I rode you quite hard at our first meeting. I considered you to be a pointless mountain stroller or, what is even worse, for a billeting officer of the loud groups calling themselves summer holidaymakers. I did not know you, and I did you an injustice — but you will also approve of my caution. I want to protect my mountain people, I do not want, for the sake of a few miserable marks, to drive the quiet ease from their plateau, and to have the peace stolen from their houses and from their hearts.

There are sanatoriums of the soul, health resorts for sick hearts. But their only remedies are simplicity and stillness. Hence they must remain isolated, otherwise their atmosphere loses its healing power, is corrupted, and infects on top of that those who were previously healthy." —

Stein liked philosophising a lot. But he was at the same time pious to the heart. And he tended his piety with the villagers too.

He practised the greatest conceivable influence on all the residents of the quiet peak. Nothing happened against his wishes, everything happened on his advice. That was also quite natural; for any strong individual, consciously or unconsciously, exercises an autocracy over the surrounding weaker natures. Stein, however, also deserved the trust of his people. He was everything to them — teacher, doctor, judge, friend and confidante, authority, and to a certain degree also pastoral worker. I have seen him in the practise of all these offices. —

# Mountain Peace

Strangely enough, the boy who had lied to his mother broke his arm a few days after the lie. He was an audacious little lad who liked climbing. The boy lay wailing on his mother's bed. The few people of the village were almost assembled in full strength. Stein observed the accident victim.

"On whose bed are you lying?", he asked him.

"On my mother's!"

"Who will take care of you now?"

"My mother!"

"Who bewails your misfortune the most of all people?"

"My mother!"

"So your mother loves you and is good to you! Have you always been good to her too?"

"Oh no, I lied to my mother," the boy sobbed.

"And broke your arm," Stein added; "be happy that it turned out thus; some of those who lie break their neck as a result. Take note, and everyone else take note too!"

That was a powerful admonishment.

Soon afterwards, Stein examined the injured arm, set it, put a splint on it, and bandaged it up. I was astonished at the calmness and expertise with which he performed the operation. Only when the boy screamed loudly and those present also began wailing did he turn around curtly, "Everyone get out!"

The directive was immediately obeyed. But to the boy, Stein said, "Keep screaming as much as you can! Then it will hurt less!"

When everything was dealt with, he left.

"I will probably look in on you sometime!"

On the same day, he went to the unfortunate boy four more times. And one time he hid right in front of me a bottle of raspberry juice under his jacket. —

A few days later, he was called to a sick goat. He shouted at the woman who owned it, a distressed little

121

woman, gruffly, "I have told you often enough, Katherine, you are overfeeding the animal! Now you've done it! I must take the goat in to cure it; it must keep to a diet, that is, it must not eat everything which a foolish woman puts in its fodder rack. Bring the animal to my place soon! You can borrow my black goat for milking until your animal is healthy again! — Just listen, Katherine — will you perhaps overfeed my black goat too?"

"Oh no, oh no, eh, why would I? Now then, there, the goat of the teacher! No, no, I'd rather give it nothing to eat."

"So? Will you let my black goat starve?"

"Oh, dear heavens, what is the teacher thinking! No, no, it will get everything it wants!"

"Katherine, you are incorrigible! Either nothing at all or everything! Neither a man nor a goat would endure that! But nonetheless, you shall have the black goat! But I tell you, I come over every time for the feeding. Before I am there, do not give the black goat a straw of hay! If you do not do exactly as I tell you, then I will let your animal die. You must learn care!"

"Oh, crazy, crazy no, no! I will wait then until the teacher comes for the feeding! And if he does, I will get everything ready then alone!"

The next day, I heard often to my secret amusement the discourse which Stein had with the really somewhat ponderous old woman echoing across the meadow. —

Another time two weavers who were unable to agree came to Stein.

"Lorenz brought me a mark too few from the manufacturer. He was delivering for me."

"Yes, Wenzel can talk, the manufacturer did not give me more. He is a dumb fool, Wenzel!"

"No, Lorenz is a dumb fool because he was diddled!"

"Calm down", Stein commanded, "it is a bad case! A mark is a lot of money, and the manufacturer will not want to pay it out. The mark belongs to you, Wenzel, for you earned it; but Lorenz cannot pay it out, for he had not received it. Consequently it will be sorted thus! This gentlemen here wants to hear our echo today, and I wanted to lead him to the place, but have no desire to anymore. It is not far to the place of the echo. So you will be the guide, Wenzel, and this gentleman will give you the mark you have forfeited as a tip."

That was a surprise for the three of us. Both weavers stared with open mouths for a while alternately at Stein and myself; then it came slowly, but in the same tempo from both mouths, "Brill!"

But, when I had recovered somewhat from my astonishment, I said the same thing, if also not in dialect, "Brilliant!" —

When accuser and accused had left, Stein laughed, and said, "Who is the convicted one now?"

"Essentially I am", I responded.

"Not essentially, but rather really," Stein continued. "And now, as is the fashion and is right, the grounds for the judgment — that neither of the two men can forfeit the mark, which is actually a lot of money for them, is clear. Thus a way out must be sought. I found that in you, in your wallet to be precise. You are capable of forfeiting a mark without great anguish; thus, you *can* pay; you are also guilty of an offence; thus, you *must* pay."

"Of an offence, how so?"

"When two people have something with each other on the quiet peak, then that concerns only them and me, whom they have chosen as their referee. A third must not be present for the dispute. But you were present at the negotiation without being authorised, and ought to have realised that before my judgement the openness of the process was once and for all out of the question. Hence the punishment!"

"Brilliant!", I said again, and submitted with a good mood to my sentence. When I later rejoiced at the magnificent echo, I paid my penalty for contempt of court gladly to the guide.

On the way home, I asked that man, "Now, are you completely reconciled with your antagonist again?"

The weaver looked at me in astonishment.

"Reconciled? I was never even angry!"

"But you accused Lorenz!"

"Accused? No, there I have to laugh! Lorenz is my godfather!"

"But you came with him to the teacher!"

"Well, I am always going to him when I know no way around it! Lorenz wanted to himself."

"Ah so!"

After a while, I asked further.

"How far does Lorenz go when he is delivering?"

"Well, over four miles."

"Does he have a heavy load to carry there?"

"He takes a cart, otherwise he couldn't haul it."

"He delivers for himself and you?"

"Yes, and also for lame Beate."

"And how much does he receive for his effort?"

"There? Nothing at all now! It is just a favour! I weave for him a whole day, and Beate three hours. That is all! Now then, the teacher would jump into the air if I paid for a favour." —

Almost always when I got involved in a conversation with the weavers, I recognised the enormously instructive influence of Stein. Just like today! —

Lorenz was already delivering again two weeks later. Very weary, but very pleased, he came to the schoolhouse that same evening.

"The manufacturer felt that he had given a mark to few. He must be very aware of money. He handed the mark over to me. Here it is!"

Touched, I wanted to gift the mark to the honest man. Then Stein intervened.

"Would that it be still more beautiful! Honesty is entirely natural and is its own reward. The mark belongs to nobody now. So may Beate have it, who has earned nothing the entire week because she is tormented by lumbago. Lorenz, take the mark to her now."

The man obeyed, without showing any crossness on his face. — —

Stein was also to some extent the pastoral worker in the little village. It was over four miles to the nearest church. Nevertheless, the poor mountain residents visited the church as often as they could. I thought with shame of so many big city residents who only needed to cross the street to satisfy their religious duty, and yet found the slightest cause sufficiently important to excuse their absence at the Sunday service.

Unfortunately, the two Sundays which I spent during my stay of about three weeks on the quiet peak were rained out so completely that the general going to church which I had looked forward to was unable to take place.

But God was served much and deeply, and I thought I had never been so pious, so reverent as on the quiet peak.

When evening came and the twilight sank down on the quiet little village, my mood always became quite indescribable. Where was there a sound, where was there even a distant recollection of the raucous world outside? Quietly, very quietly only, the needles of the fir trees crackled, as mysteriously, as sweetly as when a Christmas tree stands in a dark corner. And when the early moon climbed up over the dark forest, climbed up in its entire silver splendour, my soul was flooded by a a mixture of sweet delight and solemn devotion, then I stood quite still on the sparkling silver plateau and could not have wished for anything at that moment. It was so still in my soul, and yet it did not sleep.

The little cottages lay calmly by the dark edge of the forest as if under a spell of peace. Almost in the same minute, however, the doors opened, and men, women, children, and old people came out, and they strode slowly over the bright plateau. They stopped by the schoolhouse. Nobody spoke a word; everyone, however, folded their hands.

The windows of the schoolhouse stood wide open, and when everyone was assembled before the house, a pious prelude resounded slowly and solemnly into the night. It sounded like a fresh evening breeze which wafted the day's last drops of sweat from the forehead, like a fervent and yet irresistibly powerful admonition, "Lift your hearts!"

After the playing, the congregation sang a hymn. When I heard the song for the first time, my eyes filled with tears, and a grateful, joyous thought moved my heart:

> Dear God, even in these loud, hard-hearted, pleasure-seeking times, your omnipotence and love creates the quiet peak on which your praise rings out, simple and pious like in the days of your patriarchs! —

After hymn, Stein placed a cross in the open window, and stepped amidst the congregation himself. Before the cross, he said a prayer aloud. The latter always made reference to the events of the past day, and was adapted to the understanding and the feelings of the people. I considered this prayer, spoken under the stars of the open sky and in sight of the homely cottages, to be a powerful means of education for those whom Stein served. I will write down one such prayer from memory, that which Stein spoke on the evening of the day in which the boy had an accident:

> Good God, we are poor people, but you are our father! You are very fond of us, and we love you back! In love we pray to you, and in love we thank you for the favours of the past day and of all days!

> If we were impatient or even furious with our work today, if the earnings were too small for us and we thought to little of You, then we rue this heartily, and beg You to forgive us with mercy and make us better every day!

> We also ask You to make the injured arm of Peter well again, and forgive him his lie as his mother and all of us forgive him. Also make our schoolteacher clever and good so that he can help us when we need him!

> To Frieder, Heinrich, Anna, and Luise who have died, give, oh Lord, eternal peace, also all for whom we should otherwise still pray!

> But send us Your holy angel tonight, and lead us once from this quiet peak to Your eternal heights! Amen.

"Our Father!" — The entire congregation spoke together, and I too.

\*\*\*

The last day! The day after tomorrow, I must be home!

I had always, as much as I also take pleasure in the holidays, returned to my work without a murmur, yes, gladly and joyfully, when the free time was over. Why is this time so difficult for me? —

I have breakfast with Stein, bread and milk as always. Nobody speaks a word, one hardly looks at the other too.

On the windowpanes, fine rain is spraying, "Just the right weather for taking leave."

After breakfast, I say, "Now I must go!"

Stein nods, and fetches my bundle which he has packed himself. Then he calls his wife. She begins crying loudly; but Stein leaves the room. A few minutes later, I stand with him before the door. It does not take long before the entire congregation is assembled for the farewell. The men gaze on earnestly, the women and children are crying. Finally I free myself and go. Stein accompanies me for a piece.

I want to thank him, but he cuts my words off. He has also accepted no other payment for the accommodation than a small sum which I asked him to use for the people in the village.

From the end of the meadowed plateau, I send one last, melancholy farewell to those remaining behind. Then the forest envelops us, and we walk for a stretch, still wordlessly. It seems to me as if something were stuck in my throat.

Then Stein finally begins to talk.

"I have experienced many bitter things out in the world," he says, "and I did not think that I would once more come into closer relations with someone from below. Sometimes it goes quite wonderfully. I considered you to be someone like they all are, and like those I do not like to tolerate. At the time of the plants incident, I hated you. I had intended to embarrass you, and then chase you out of the house. But I soon saw that the cuttings were not familiar to you, and when you then confessed everything — you know because of the children — then — well, I did not chase you away just then. I did not rue it. You have not disturbed our mountain peace. You should come again!"

With that, he stopped walking. I seized his hand, and pressed it firmly, "You good man! You do not know how happy I was with you, how much I have obtained from you in my state of mind! God reward you! And next year, I will come again!"

He kissed me on the forehead, and went. When he vanished at the turn in the forest path, I leant on the nearest fir tree and cried.

\*\*\*

I came back the following year, and also many a year after that. It was as if the desire to roam away into the distance had completely died in me. I made no holiday plans anymore like I had previously, but soon after the close of school I buckled up my backpack and made my pilgrimage to the quiet peak. Often an acquaintance asked me about my summer accommodation, but I have not betrayed the quiet refuge to anyone until the present day. It is not the blatant self-interest which imposes this silence on me, but the fear that peace, the best possession of the mountain residents, would be lost to them, and they would receive nothing for it but a supplementary income which would not even outweigh their own newly growing, increased needs, not to think at all of the ideal possessions which would be sacrificed. —

I was always received on the quiet peak with hearty joy. The entire little village always made me welcome. And the welcome greeting was then always followed by glorious days of quiet happiness.

Stein became closer and closer to me from year to year. And once — the occasion is too sacred to me, it should be in my heart and not on paper — he called me his friend. The word fills me still today with proud happiness, for it was no empty word with him.

On the afternoon of the same day, I remained alone. Stein was writing. In the evening, however, he brought a light into my little room, and a few inscribed pages.

"There," he said, "friends should know each other entirely. You do not know me entirely yet. On these pages, I have written what you as my friend must know. Read it, and look me openly in the face tomorrow as always!"

He left. Trembling with excitement, I grasped the pages, and read:

There is much land between a child's cradle of ebony and the wooden chair on which an old man sits. Much land, and much time! And it is also a long way from a gaming room in which you place your money and estate, family's fortune and own happiness, honour, and life on a few cards, to a quiet forest path on which the foot makes a detour because it does not want to trample on a worm. Infinitely much grace is a part of it when an eye, which itself does not twitch anymore before the suicidal weapon because sin and shame paralyses the eyelid, learns once more to light up happily at the sight of a white meadow flower.

I have traversed the land from the ebony cradle to the wooden chair, I wandered the path from the gaming room to the forest path, and it is my eyes which once dared God, and whose eyelashes now fall on the cheek when praying. I was rich once, and now I am poor, once a distinguished man who called himself doctor, and of whom greatness was prophesied, and am now a mountain schoolmaster whom nobody knows; but I was also once a great rogue, and am now an old man who has found his peace.

If I wanted to give an account of my life, then it would be a long tale, a tale which a good man would have to feel disgusted at reading. So I will make it short.

I am from a noble house. The residents of the quiet peak only know me under the name Stein. My parents were wealthy land-owners, and everything possible was done for the education of my sister and myself. I can look back on a pure childhood and on a good attitude in the time of my youth. I praise God for that and believe that I have those pure years of my youth to thank for my happy old age. I was diligent, all the world called me gifted, and thus I passed my exams with honour at the elite high school, and made good progress in my university studies. I pursued the social sciences, but also became intimate with the subjects of natural history. I can say that I was an avid student. I obtained my doctorate at a comparatively early age, but nevertheless did not yet abandon the college, instead continuing to study. My circumstances allowed me to proceed with my studies from pure idealism. Up to then everything was beautiful and good. My father, an officer, certainly grumbled over his only son whom he called a "stay-at-home and pigskin hero", but my mother looked with inward delight at me, and my sister, who blossomed into a lovely young lady loved me enthusiastically.

Then my father fell in a duel.

A single sentence is able to report the incident, it also happened in a single second. But the sorrow which followed it filled years — evil years!

When a misfortune encounters a family whose limbs stand very close, it has an effect like a bomb-shell which falls in closed ranks — it wounds everyone.

Oh, when I think of my mother!

She was so pious, she believed firmly that only after a blissful death could a blessed eternity follow. Now father had died in a duel! And she had loved father so ardently!

He had sent a look to heaven before he parted. Onto that did the hope of her love clasp! Even today I hear her sobbing prayer, "Lord, let it have been a look of sinning remorse!"

Where is a son who shares such a sorrow, who does not drink from the wounds of such a maternal heart the strength to be a solace to the poor woman until the end, a son who has the heart to prepare new woe for such a mother?

Here! — I am! —

The bullet which bored through the chest of my father had also struck the soul of the son. Since the death of my father, I did not pray anymore, and if I ever looked to heaven, it happened with a sullen eye. Along with the prayers, I stopped my work. I found no enjoyment in it anymore. I brooded over it. And with all the brooding, a crust formed over my heart. No sympathy sprung up in me for the fallen officer, I scolded him to myself as the disloyal corrupter of our happiness. But worse yet, I offended my mother.

To start with, her sorrow tore up my soul, and her constant, half despairing, half hoping prayers daily brought my young heart new, heavy distress. And above all the woe and the unhappiness of the days, the youth in me rose up, and the lamenting became odious to me. And once I scolded the ideas of my mother, which I called all too orthodox. Then she looked at me with deep sadness. From this day on, I saw no more tears from her, but her pale face told me more than tears and words, and I became still more embittered.

Finally, I did not think I could bear it any longer, and avoided the house as much as I could. But when you do not work and are also not happy at home, you mostly become a loafer. Thus I was too. I learnt all at once card playing, and ran around all the taverns. I behaved somewhat like someone who tries to numb his bad conscience. Only, that it was not the conscience with me, but the thought of father and mother which seemed unbearable to me. My ease had been too cheerful. Now I was shocked out of it, I was not strong enough to be steadfast.

Then a new turn entered my life — in the midst of the loneliness of my heart, love struck me like a blinding happiness. Only slowly did I, deprived of happiness, get to grips with it. But then I was blissfully happy. She was middle class, but she seemed like an angel to me. I do not want to fall into raptures here; I just want to offer one thing to characterise my condition.

I once knelt down before my mother, and said, "Mother, now I am in love, I understand you! I am in love more than you were in love! If just the thought came to me that my only one could arrive at eternal bliss, I would go mad!" — —

What else is there to say? One thing — my faith in my heart's love was a mistake. — —

Now comes the part of my tale of which I said it would, told in-depth, awaken loathing in the reader. That is why I want to say in short, I was an unfathomably reckless man. I forced myself to vice. My movement towards the slippery slope was an abrupt leap which had to lead by necessity to a long, heavy fall.

I want to confess one more thing. The most fateful of my vices was the rage for gaming. One day my mother said, "My son, your sister and I, we still have three thousand talers, do not take it from us!"

Four weeks after that, the money had been gambled away.

At the time, I loaded the pistol, and set it to my forehead. A black veil was placed over my eyes. I pulled the trigger.

The pistol failed to go off.

At the same moment, my sister plunged into the room, "Mother is dying!" —

God's work! — — —

My mother did not die. God inspired me with good words to preserve her. A great hope was capable of holding up a fleeing soul. — —

To close! My sister went into an abbey. She had always been a quiet soul. She had found her happiness and her salvation. —

I, however, became schoolmaster on the quiet peak. How did it come about? Previously, a weaver who could read and write had given a few lessons here off his own bat. Nobody knew about the quiet peak. Then a government official strayed here, and pressed for a different person to fill the role. I learnt of it. I had meanwhile again been leading a respectable life in a private office, and received the position through an advocate to whom I expressed my and my mother's desire for withdrawing from the world. Nobody else knows where I went.

Soon after the terrible and yet gracious night in which a light went on in my soul, God begrudged me the offering of a great happiness to my mother. I sought out one of the seconds who had been at my father's death, and questioned him. Until then I had avoided these people as our worst enemies. The man was shaken by my request; but he swore an oath that father's last look had been of consuming fervour, and he had said at the same time the name "Jesus". By this news, my mother was healed. —

I took her with me to the quiet peak. The people revered her. I will not say how I cherished her. She was happy up to her pious death. —

I later took a wife. I had become a mountain schoolmaster, and she was healthy in body and soul. Hence!

I seldom still think about the world. In an attic are a few cartons with books. I threw the attic key in the creek. I have tried a few times over the years to spring the lock, but always desisted from it again. I have up here other sciences to tend to. —

I pray and work. I know that God has forgiven me, for he has given me peace.

This is my story! Remain my friend!

When I had read these few words, my eyes were hot. The next morning, I said to Stein, "I love you!" —

I wanted to return the pages to him; but he said, "Keep them! You are a writer of tales! Write up about me and the quiet peak if you want! Perhaps it can serve someone; but it won't harm me!" —

I have written it up in this little book. If I go to my friend a year from now, I will show him it. And what he says to me in the way of criticism, I will note word for word.

# FORGE FIRE
# (A CHARACTER STUDY)

The forge fire mostly burns slowly. It puffs away. Dead ash lies over it and only occasionally lets a golden spark shimmer through.

Then little Jack lies bored in the large, black, wall niche, while his father, the smith, keeps his tools and iron bars ready, and on his left side are the bellows under which the fire glimmers. So still does the boy lie, his head placed on his right arm, that you might think he was sleeping. But he is not sleeping, he peers out under his more than half-closed eyelids at the fire. He is lying in wait.

He lies in wait for the fire, and for his father, the smith. When the latter seizes a piece of iron with his tongs and approaches the fire with it, the boy leaps up straightaway, quickly, as if driven by a great excitement, and now has his eyes wide-open and directed at the fire.

"Draw! Draw! Huh! Ah!"

The fire flares up high. It illuminates the pale, handsome face of the boy, it radiates in his black eyes, and you do not know whether the fire or his eyes gleams the more.

But when the smith then steps to the anvil with the glowing red iron, and lets the hammer fall on it so that the sparks fly, then the boy is out of the smithy at the third or fourth blow.

Thus also today.

Little Jack looks around before the house. He sees his grandmother in the garden. She is weeding. Since he knows nothing better right then, he steps over to her.

"Are you wanting to help me, little Jack?", the old woman asks.

"Help? Me?"

The questioning response comes from the boy's mouth like an astonished, wounded pride so that his grandmother gets annoyed at having caused it first. So she says soothingly, "Just let it be, little Jack, I just said it without thinking! But stay a little with me!"

The old woman continues assiduously weeding, but the boy stands upright and gazes. As far as the windmills, or the bluish grey line of the horizon, or still further, who knows!

The brittle back of his grandmother bends incessantly over the vegetable bed, the stiff fingers search incessantly for ragwort and sow thistles, and annoyance incessantly passes through her grey head over the question, "Are you wanting to help me, little Jack?"

Little Jack is not interested in work. His mother was a princess, certainly not one with castles and silk dresses, but certainly one anyway. The people in the village had all called her that, and yet were not nice to her at all.

She had come to the village with a wandering troupe. She had been very pale and very sad, but also very beautiful. Then the son of old Katherina was smitten. Soon the neighbours had hissed in her ear, "He is running after the actress", and she, the mother, had noted it even before the neighbours. She had warned him, and cried and prayed much, but it had been no use. And one day he had stormed into the room, excited and full of jubilation, that usually so quiet son.

"Mother, she will be mine! I told her everything, everything, mother! Then tears came into her beautiful eyes, and she reached her hand out to me. I want to have a home, she said at the same time. Is that not a great fortune, mother?"

Katherina had not known whether it was a great fortune, but she had submitted to it. Her son had taken the strange woman, and led her to the smithy as his wife. How the people had talked and reviled everything, Katherina had long since forgotten. It is good that she forgot it, for it was a loveless talk.

But the pale woman herself she cannot forget, although she had remained almost completely foreign to her in the eleven years in which they had both lived in the same house. She was and remained a stranger.

Of the distant land from which she came, she spoke little, but always thought of it. She never smiled. Only when the boy was born and she saw how similar he was to her did she rejoice aloud.

From then on, her life belonged to the child. She dedicated to it all her labour, all her worry. The mother-in-law had to take care of the housekeeping. Her husband was content, he revered her as a fortune he did not deserve. She barely loved him, but she sometimes caressed his head gently, and said, "You are so kind and so loyal!"

She spoke with the boy all day, but always in a foreign tongue. The grandmother did not understand a word of it; but it must have been strange things which they both discussed. Sometimes they both cried, then they exulted aloud again, the boy loudest of all, and mostly they dreamt under the blue sky.

Paul Keller

"Leave them, she is telling him stories", the son said, and was industrious from early to late. He never urged her to work, and still less the child.

"She is not meant for that", he said.

Then the woman died. The strong smith stood loudly lamenting by the coffin of his wife, his son soundless and without tears. When they returned home from the cemetery, the boy clambered up on his deeply bowed father, and said, "Don't cry! It is all nonsense; she will come again."

He waited for this return. But when he always waited in vain, he became quite still and taciturn. He lay for hours next to the forge fire, and stared at the glimmering coals. The taciturn smith did not speak with him, but he looked over to him nearly every minute. —

All that goes through the grandmother's head as she is weeding, and that is not strange at all, for she thinks almost always of the same thing. Now she straightens up.

"Tell me, little Jack, why do you always run out of the smithy when your father is hammering iron."

"I only go when he is hammering red-hot iron."

"And why only with the red-hot iron?"

"Don't you know?"

The old woman shook her head.

The boy remained silent for a while, then he said, "I will tell you a folktale. Pay attention, grandmother!

There was once something very beautiful, something that was even more beautiful than gold. Gold is dead and only shimmers quite weakly, but this beautiful thing lived and gleamed and sparkled, ah, so gloriously! And when the storm came, it grew, grew quite high, and blazed up and gleamed as brightly as the sun.

Then a man came who had an iron in his hand. With the iron he caught the beautiful thing, and when he had caught it, he struck it dead. For the iron's sake! —

Do you know, grandmother, what that is?"

The grandmother nodded.

"I think, the forge fire."

"The forge fire — yes, it could be the forge fire," the boy responded animatedly, "I thought that at first, when I thought of the folktale, but actually, grandmother, that solution is too dumb. It must be something else, grandmother, something similar, but much better. Do you know what, grandmother?"

The old woman shook her head.

"I do not know either," the boy said sadly, "but I guess that it is something — with me. Oh, if mother lived she would certainly know. But mother is dead."

The old woman straightened up in shock.

"Don't look at me so fearfully, grandmother, I know now that mother is dead." — —

A year later, the grandmother died. Father and son walked home together from the cemetery.

"The pastor made a very beautiful speech, and praised your good grandmother a lot, don't you think, little Jack?"

"Oh yes, father, but he forgot the best and saddest thing."

"And that would be?"

"You see, since mother is dead, I have only been able to tell grandmother the folktales which I thought up. She did not understand everything, by any means, but she listened so well. Now she is dead, and you do not have the time for me."

"Be still, little Jack, I will always have time for you now if you want to tell me something."

And they stepped into the deserted smithy. — —

In the village tavern there is a local council sitting. The farmers had discussed Steffen, the son of the rogue Matheis, who had lost his father, and was now orphaned so that the village had to taken him on as a "parish child".

With the farmers, almost everything is arranged according to tradition, even charity. According to tradition, the farmer places a two pfennig piece in the collection bag on Sunday; according to tradition, he gives to the poor his gifts of bread, milk, and potatoes; according to tradition, he places his hand heavily and irremovably on the money box. A "parish child", however, is a rare case for whom the customs have no definite solution at hand.

There was hence today an awful lot of racking of brains in the village tavern, and racking brains is not everybody's thing. It was still most comfortable to complain. So they complained over the rogue Matheis who had liked drinking schnaps, which was the cause of this death which was so awkward for the parish, and grumbled over Steffen who was no use, in fact no use at all for anything.

A little away, by the door, sat the smith, serious and taciturn as ever. He probably did not know himself why he had gone to the council sitting today. Thus he was also only listening with half an ear to what the farmers were bragging about.

"He pinches apples and pears," the leaseholder of the allée complained. "As if such a rogue had need to eat fruit."

"And he lamed my Nero," complained another, and nobody contradicted him, although everybody hated and feared the dog as a nasty cur.

"Steffen is slovenly beyond measure," a third made himself heard. "The good jacket which my boy still wore on Sundays two years ago, and which I gifted to him, he has torn up in the space of half a year."

"He is supposed also to eat an incredible amount," miserly Krüger sighed.

"And he is lazy," Bader cried, "lazy like the smith's little Jack."

Bader had sounded the words out shrilly with his unpleasant, piercing voice loudly into the room. A momentary, eerily touching silence followed those words. All looks were directed to the table by the door, to the smith. He was sitting there with bowed head, his eyes directed at the table from which the voice came, stiffly as if the heard affront had paralysed him.

Then suddenly life comes into the massive figure, the smith straightens up, he pushed the table aside like a child's toy so that the glasses on it fall over, and all of a sudden stands in the middle of the room.

"Who," he calls with loud, but trembling voice into the room, "who is saying such a thing about my child?"

The farmers move closer together, and Bader giggles sheepishly with his bright, unpleasant voice. There it is made clear to the smith.

"You, Bader, you? You, miserable man, you revile my — child? — That is your misfortune, Bader — your — misfortune!"

All the blood streams into the smith's face, his eyes seem bloodshot; with a violent jerk, he pulls the table behind which Bader sat to the side, and with a groaning sound, like an irritable predator, he wants to plunge on the offensive man. Then he is seized, and held firmly by a dozen hands.

"Hold him, hold the raging man!"

"Let me go, — he has — made malicious remarks about my child!"

With a giant effort, the smith works against his assailers, in vain, he is incapable of shedding the many sinewy hands.

"Let me go! My child, my little Jack!"

And again he struggles in vain. Bader, protected by so many arms, feels completely secure. As a result, his impudence also grows again.

"What did I say?", he shouts, "I said the truth! The entire parish knows that the smith's little Jack is the most worthless rascal in the village. He stand around all day long, gapes at the clouds, and talks mad stuff. And he learnt all that from his mother, who also —".

"Bader!" The one word sounds both like a lament, and like a terrible threat. But he who has started does not stray.

"Who, I say, was also lazy and not very clever and —"

"Wretched man!"

Three or four farmers stagger towards the wall, the smith has gotten his right arm free, he quickly seizes a beer glass which stands on the nearby table, and throws it with terrible fury at Bader's head. With a scream, overflowing with blood, the struck man slides down the wall, and does not stir his limbs anymore.

"Hold him. Strike him dead, the murderer! Lead him to the court! Take care that he does not kill a second!"

The cries ring out in horror and confusion. The timid men step back from the smith.

But he stands motionless in the midst of his accusers and oppressors. His face is ashen, his pithy arms hang down slackly by his torso.

"It had — to be — thus, — my little Jack and — my — my — poor — wife — slandered! — Then, — tie me up!"
— — —

It was night. The village street lay as if dead, only the autumn wind was making its play on it with dry twigs and withered leaves. In the sky, black clouds hung full of cold rain.

Only in the tavern did light still shimmer through between the badly closed shutters. The farmers, excited to an extreme by the day's bloody scene, saw in it a favourable opportunity to remain sitting, chatting, and drinking.

Now they had already been discussing for hours the same stuff, and had not yet become absolutely weary of it. Their imagination, usually lame and sluggish, was all of a sudden animated, busy; combination followed on combination, and if these farmers had been permitted to play with providence, it would gone badly enough for the poor smith.

Not that the smith would have been especially against them! He was to the contrary a diligent crafts-man who inflicted harm on nobody, certainly also did not talk in his taciturn, serious way for the pleasure of anyone. But he had brought a foreign element into the village, the foreign woman who was so entirely different from the other women, noble in her way, amenable to nobody. And the boy was like her. That had nourished an unease towards the smith in the ponderous disposi-tions of the farmers, an unease which now all of a sudden received an outlet. On top of that came the urge which an unusual occurrence always exercises on a dreary life, a beneficial excitement which can be enter-tained without having to have the slightest fear for oneself.

The kerosene lamp burned dimly red in the tobacco smoke haze of the barroom. The farmers stared com-fortably before themselves into the smoke of their pipes. Nobody looked around. Otherwise they could easily have observed large, dark eyes which were gazing in through the gap in the window shutters.

Outside by the window, drenched by rain and shaken by the storm, little Jack was crouching. He was freezing, and trembling all over. But he did not stir. Attentive, with burning eyes, he had now already been gazing for two hours through the tavern window. And he pressed his ear again and again to the damp cold windowpane to learn what the farmers were talking about. In vain, the storm clattered the window too much, and the voices of the farmers echoed in confusion indistinctly from the room. Then someone for whom the fumes might have become too much opened the window. If needed, little Jack could still move to the side. He held firmly and with great difficulty to the vine trellis which was by the wall. The farmer meanwhile soon liberated him from his uncomfortable position by stepping back into the room.

Now little Jack could also hear more easily through the open window the content he wished so eagerly to learn. The doggedness of the farmers in the treatment of their theme came to his aid.

"Bader is certainly dying," one was just saying, "the doctor from the town said so."

"No," another said, "he only said that Bader is in danger."

"Danger, hm, you know it! Doctors always say that when they don't have any other advice and don't want to reveal the naked truth straightaway. Bader is dying, take note!"

"And, Schulze, do you really think then, the smith —"

"But, that is quite clear! My uncle has told me many hundreds of times — you know the story of the butcher Sepp. The butcher Sepp wanted to take his master's daughter as his wife; but because he was a dissolute fellow, the master did not want him for a son-in-law, and finally chased him out of the house when he became insistent. Then Sepp had in fury waited in ambush on the master that evening, and stabbed him — with his butcher's knife."

The farmers shuddered, and moved closer together, although they had heard the story already countless times.

"Well, and do you see what happened to the butcher Sepp? It came out, and he was beheaded. Why? He committed a 'murder of revenge', the lords of the court said, and for that there is the guillotine every time. Now, and our smith? Bader insulted him, just like Sepp was insulted by his master, then the smith fell into a fury just like Sepp did, and — and he committed a murder of revenge, just like Sepp did, and that is why he will also be just like Sepp —"

"Beheaded!", the dignified chorus complete it.

Then a shrill, earsplitting cry sounds from the window. The farmers start as if struck by lightning.

"Bader! Bader! For heaven's sake, Bader! Have you heard — Bader! He has died, and revealed himself to us, and he screamed just like before when he was struck. That is a misfortune! — Bader, Bader! If only the window had not been open! Who opened it? A misfortune — Bader!"

While the farmers are moaning and lamenting, little Jack lies half unconscious on the ground under the window. The damp, cold earth brings him to. He rises laboriously, and creeps away from there with shuffling steps. The farmers hear his weary, shuffling steps, and shudder. Nobody dares go to the window. But little Jack drags himself away as far as the smithy.

There an impenetrable night surrounds the boy, but he does not need any light, he finds what he is looking for in the darkness. It rings quietly under the tools of the smith, then the boy steps back out into the street.

He creeps cautiously down the village street, often pausing and listening. But nothing sounds in his ear but the whistling of the autumn storm, the groaning of the wind-bowed trees, and the rustling of the dry leaves.

Somewhat in the middle of the village stands a small, low house, the fire station. The little house serves a triple purpose. It received its name from an old, unusable fire hose which is preserved in it, then the bodies of strangers and suicides were concealed in it, and finally

147

it served as interim safekeeping for those arrested who are to be lead away to the quite distant county seat at the next opportunity.

Little Jack stops at the little house. He places himself close under the barred window, holds his breath, and listens. No human sound! Then the boy jumps high up by the wall, seizes an iron bar and does not let go, although the iron cuts terribly into his flesh. His groping feet finally find a narrow ledge on which they can support themselves.

"Father!"

No answer.

"Father!"

Then it stirs in the fire station.

"Who is calling? Is it you, little Jack?"

"Yes, father, it's me! Listen quick, father, before the guard comes. The farmers in the tavern said you had committed a revenge murder just like the butcher Sepp, and hence you will — but don't be too frightened, father — hence you will be — beheaded."

The boy listened timidly for the answer.

"That is nonsense, little Jack, I will not be beheaded."

"Not beheaded? A—a—ah! But — really — not?"

"Quite certainly not, little Jack, the farmers are dumb."

"Very dumb", the boy said with conviction.

"But I will be imprisoned, perhaps for a long, long time!"

"Imprisoned? You — father? That would be horrible! To be imprisoned is as bad as dying! The dead are also merely imprisoned in their graves. No, no, no, father, that must not be, you must be free, free as the fire when the wind blows in! You must get out!"

"That I cannot do, little Jack!"

"But you can! Go away, father, sparks are flying!"

There is a tinkling of bursting glass in the prison window.

"What did you do, little Jack?"

"I have brought the files, your best files — but quiet — the guard — don't be frightened if I scream, father, I will do it merely so —"

"Who is there by the fire station?"

Quickened steps approach the jail.

Then — a horrified, shrill scream, and a second and a third.

The steps fell silent, as if who they originated from were paralysed by fright, then sounds, at first sounding in babbling shock, then screeching horrified shouts of fear, "Bader, dead Bader! He is with his murderer! Help! Bader!"

And in racing haste, the guard runs down the village street.

The boy listens, then he breaks out into a giggling laughter.

"That was good", he said.

"What was that, little Jack?"

"I have driven the guard away. He is exactly as stupid as the farmers. When I scream, he thinks it is the ghost of Bader, and becomes afraid."

"Bader? — He — is — not — yet — dead, — little Jack?"

"Dead?"

The boy pauses. Then he says quickly, "Certainly not, it is surely quite well with him."

From the prison, there came a deep sigh.

"Bader must not die, you hear, little Jack."

"No, he must not", the boy says.

It remains still for a while again, only the heavy breaths of the smith come from the fire station. The boy notices his father's unease, but he does not ask about it.

Paul Keller

Then he begins again, "Take the files, father, and file through the grating! You must get out!"

"It won't work, little Jack."

"It — won't — work? It must work! Just file, that it will work."

"And then, little Jack?"

"Then we will move far away. Do you know where? To mother's land. Oh, you don't know how beautiful it is in mother's land, but I know. File, father!"

"I won't do it!"

"You won't do it? You must do it! Otherwise you'll be locked away, you said that yourself."

"Yes, little Jack, but I want to take my punishment."

"You want — *want* — to be locked away — *want* — father?"

"Yes, little Jack!"

Then the boy lets go, and springs down from the ledge.

"Where are you, little Jack?"

No answer.

"Little Jack! Little Jack! Little Jack! Answer me!"

The smith calls the name with a loud voice, but only the autumn wind answers him, cutting coldly in through the shattered window.

"Little Jack! Little Jack! Little Jack! —"

He crouches motionless on the damp earth, and leans his head wearily against the rough wall of the fire station. A sorrow cuts through his young soul. In the middle of the chasing, cold autumn mist, nothing freezes but his heart, and that freezes with his thoughts of the man who sits inside the prison and — is his father.

"Little Jack! Little Jack! Where are you?" — —

Hour upon hour passes. The black clouds scurry ghostily across the sky, and the storm plays with them and plays with the leaves on the ground, and plays with the freezing child by the fire station. —

Towards morning, little Jack stands up. His limbs want to fail him, but he forces himself.

"Father!", he calls from below.

"Little Jack, are you there again? Where were you though, little Jack!"

"Throw the files out again, father. It is better!"

"That is true, my dear, — there! But now tell me where you were."

"I was here!"

"Here?"

"Yes, here! It was very hard! The wind is so cold, and then I hurt somewhat, and then I had so much to think about. Listen to me, father! Before when you said you *wanted* to be locked away, it felt in my heart as if I did not love you as much anymore."

"Little Jack!"

"Don't be angry, father! You see, mother could not have lived locked away, and I could not either. But you — you can, you even want it, and that hurts me. Do you know when I loved you the most, father?"

"When?", comes soundlessly from the cell.

"Last night, when I heard that you had struck down Bader. You seemed so strong to me, father, as strong as a hero. But then you spoke of punishment, and that sounded as if you were condemning your own deed."

The boy paused; he awaited an answer. But since none came, he continued, "Now I was thinking all night, and now I know that every man acts and thinks as he must. You cannot help it, father, that you want to re-main locked away, and I am fond of you again."

A pause. Then the smith sobs, "Little Jack, what will become of you?"

"Of me? You see, father, mother would not have asked that. She would simply have gotten out, and looked after me. But you, you remain inside, must remain inside, and have such a soft heart, and will worry about me every day. That will be a great sorrow."

"A very great sorrow, little Jack!"

"And it is also hard for me. Do you know what I want to become? An author, father, a great author! You will not believe at all how many stories I know, as beautiful as mother's. And I thought up all the stories myself, and wanted to write them down in large books that all men could read. That is also why I did not ever want to work. What can you think at work? That you do nothing wrong, nothing else! What a shame that is though for thinking and for the time! And now I will have to go work for a farmer, and will not become a great author, but a farm labourer."

"Little Jack!", the smith cries out, "my poor, poor, dear little Jack!" And he cries bitterly.

The boy stands quite still, then he suddenly says, "Father, I must go, I am freezing so much all of a sudden. Farewell and come back soon! I will wait here for you!"

"Little Jack, my child, my son! Just one word! Little Jack, little Jack, little Jack!"

The prisoner did not receive an answer anymore.

\*\*\*

The next morning, the smith was led away. The village street by the fire station and the adjoining garden was filled completely with people. A wave of blood shot into the smith's countenance when he left his prison and saw the crowd. How the curiosity directed at his suffering hurt him, hurting more almost than the schadenfreude which slipped off his sullen fury. But everything passes; even behind the smith, the hissing sounds of his former neighbours and acquaintances faded away.

# Forge Fire (A Character Study)

When the smith stood before the court, Bader was long since out of all danger of dying. Nevertheless he had been injured badly enough. With consideration for the severe injury, but also the extenuating circumstances, the smith was sentenced to six months in jail. The residents of the village were greatly disillusioned at the news. —

When little Jack had returned to the smithy after staying awake all night by the fire station, he had immediately crept into the large, black wall niche, and had cowered in the old, familiar place. Nevertheless he did not sleep, but gazed with great, blazing eyes over to the place where the forge fire usually was. How dead and black the ashes over there now lay! It looks as black, the boy thought, as in his heart.

In the morning, it became light in the smithy, the boy did not stir, voices resounded before the house, little Jack did not hear them. Then suddenly the village street roars like breakers; a racket occurs out on the street which sounds dreadful in the quiet smithy.

"Oh God, they are taking father!"

Little Jack hastens to the hindmost, completely dark part of the niche. There it is deepest night, but the boy nevertheless closes his eyes, and presses both hands fast against his ears. Thus he is completely motionless, for a long time yet after the racket outside has long since faded away.

Towards evening, little Jack gets up, and walks down the village. He sheds no tears as he closes up the homely smithy, he is merely very pale. He goes to ask, to ask for work, he, little Jack.

"If grandmother knew," he thinks.

He stops before the big homestead of the head of the parish. The mayor really must accept him, but little Jack thinks of his tale of the butcher Sepp. Then he balls his fist, and he walks past.

At the end of the village lives a peculiar man. He resides with his old housekeeper alone on his little property, works early and late, does not speak more than ten words the entire day, and converses with no man.

"He has a guilty conscience," the people say succinctly, and avoid him.

Little Jack goes to him. An inner feeling urges him there. He meets the strange man before the house. The man looks wordlessly and questioningly at the boy.

"I am asking you for work and board, Senzel," little Jack says.

The man addressed looks at him again wordlessly; then he nods as a sign that he has understood the address.

"But I — can — not — work," little Jack stutters on.

"You can tend livestock," the taciturn man then says, "go inside!"

Thus little Jack was taken on. — —

The October sun stood in the sky. A mild wind was still blowing over the stubble and playing with the half withered grass and the last flowers of the field margins. Little Jack lay stretched out on the field margin. Probably more than thirty steps from him lay a whip, and on the field over there the cows were grazing.

Little Jack gazed up at the clear autumn sky, and listened with pleasure to the clattering of a nearby windmill.

The work now did not seem at all so horrible to him as he had thought at first. His four charges were well-behaved animals who respected with great conscientiousness the boundaries of the quite narrowly enclosed meadow, his employer gave him the entire week long neither a good nor a bad word, in short, little Jack was quite content with his lot. He had time to dream and to think, almost as much time as at home in the smithy.

# Forge Fire (A Character Study)

From time to time, little Jack raises his head and gazed down to the village as if he wants to have a look at whether the smith's cottage, whose gable protrudes from the yellow crowns of the trees, still stands. Since that evening, he has never been in it; the mayor demanded the key from him.

The cottage stands just as always. Little Jack nods amiably at it, and then in the exercise of his office, he sends an occasional side-glance to the cows.

"Everything in order!", he says, and continues dreaming. After a while he whistles. Behind on the back-slope a ragged dog raises its muzzle from the mouse hole in which it was sniffing, and listens. He was given to little Jack half for help, half for company in the meadows, but pays as little attention to the cows as his young master, instead adhering to his passions just like the latter. Now a second whistle rings out across the field margin, which finally causes the dog to set off at an easy trot in the direction of the whistle.

He stops right before little Jack, and wags his tail ever so slightly. Soft dirt still hangs on his muzzle, the bristly hairs are half grey and half black.

"A shabby fellow," little Jack grumbles to himself, "but someone all the same. Lie down, Nero!"

The dog lies down close next to the boy who rips up a handful of grass and cleans the dog's muzzle with it.

"So, and now look at me and listen! I want to tell you something, something which can interest you."

The dog meanwhile does not gaze at the boy, but blinks over at the slope.

"Beast, dumb, ungrateful one!"

And little Jack gives the dog a slap so that it flinches howling. Then both lie quite still, the boy and the dog. After a while, a growl! Little Jack does not stir. Renewed growling! The boy remains silent a little while, then he says, "Boring you probably, dumb cur! Would suit you quite right! But this time I'll let it pass. You are just an animal, and there are even men for whom something to eat is preferred to the most beautiful story. So listen!

There were once two dogs. One was beautiful and clever, the other was ugly and dumb, just like you! Don't growl, stupid animal, rather take quite calmly what I tell you! So just as dumb as you! The dumb dog sniffed around the entire day long in the kitchen. Sometimes it received blows, but it came again and again. You will see that it had not a trace of honour in its body. Yes, it threw itself down so far that it even ate the potatoes from the pig's trough. Don't growl, I know that you would not do the latter. But you eat mice, and that is not much better. To continue! The entire heroism of the dumb and ugly dog consisted in that at the command of its master, which I consider justified, it chased around the geese and hens which, tired of the comfortless monotony in the yard, sometimes undertook an excursion into the garden, and it tore a few feathers from the inept birds. You see, he was a quite wretched creature.

The beautiful and clever dog was quite different. It spurned begging from crumbs and crusts, instead taking now and again a sausage or suchlike, for dogs are carnivores, and it probably knew that. It decidedly did not chase hens and geese; that was too cowardly for it, for the poultry were weaker than it. Instead it was a passionate hunter. It raced the hares, and when it caught one, it bit through its neck and got a taste of the game.

That all did not suit its master at all now, and one day, when he had caught it maliciously, he beat it dreadfully with a stick.

The next hour, the dog left the homestead of its master forever. You growl because you do not understand how you could willingly give up a regularly filled milk bowl, a warm place by the stove, and a kennel filled with soft straw.

# Forge Fire (A Character Study)

Ah, Nero, if you could just understand what it is like when you have a passionate heart. You see, then you give up everything, gladly everything only so that you can be free, free! In the autumn mist, the noble animal chased across the fields, its breath panted, its eyes gleamed, and it did not think of the warm stove in the farmer's living room; it often had to go hungry, but it did not yearn for the dirty milk bowl from which all the cats lapped, and in the evening it lay in a field furrow and froze, but it did not want to go home to the cottage on which a chain rattled, but the next morning chase again, without restraint, unbound, free! And when the hunter then entered the field, and its own master shot it, when it lay bleeding on the grass, and saw how the nasty dog bared its teeth with a grin and rubbed against its master — hey, if it had had a soul like mine, then it would have rejoiced, and would have died rejoicing! —"

"Child, child, where do you know that from?"

With a jerk, little Jack is on his feet. Before him stand two elegantly clothed gentlemen. Little Jack stares at them speechlessly. Then one, a gentleman with a very dark, though friendly face, says again, "We have listened along to your entire story, my child! Your dog noticed us and growled; but you were too rapt in your telling to have heard us arriving. But now tell, from whom did you get that story?"

"The story?", little Jack asked in astonishment. "I did not get it from anyone!"

"But you must know it from someone! Or did you think it up all by yourself?"

"I have thought up entirely different stories to this one, but the dumb dog understands none better, and I have nobody else."

"Tell me, child, who you are, and tell me too one of your stories!"

Paul Keller

"I bring to your attention, Professor, that it is already getting cool, and the sun will soon go down."

"But, dear Doctor, we will not ignore such a child. What the boy told, and the way he told it, was extraordinary. Who knows what sort of genius awaits discovery here."

"Then I will walk ahead slowly," the other man, a young, gaunt man, says with a weary, nervous facial expression, and walks on. The dark man, however, sits down in the field margin, draws little Jack next to him, and says in a friendly manner, "So, now tell, and have no fear."

"Fear?", little Jack asks in astonishment, and then he narrates. At first of his mother, then of his grandmother, and then of his father. The face of the stranger twitches as with the gleam of jubilation.

"My dear, good child, there is much sadness there," he says after the telling, "but console yourself, your father will soon come home again. And now tell me one of your stories."

"I know quite a few, and I also understand them all, only one I don't understand, and yet I thought it up myself too. Grandmother also knew no better answer than I did; but you will in the end be a clever gentleman and know the answer."

"We will see," the stranger smiled. "Tell!"

And the boy narrated, "There was once something very beautiful, something that was even more beautiful than gold. Gold is dead and only shimmers quite weakly, but this beautiful thing lived and gleamed and sparkled, ah, so gloriously! And when the storm came, it grew, grew quite high and blazed up and gleamed as brightly as the sun.

Then a man came who had an iron in his hand. With the iron he caught the beautiful thing, and when he had caught it, he struck it dead. For the iron's sake!

Grandmother said it was the forge fire, and I also knew no better. But I know that there is something more to it. Something resides in me which burns thus, and is as beautiful as the fire. But it can be caught and killed. What is it?"

The stranger stared in bewilderment at the boy. Finally he said, "Child, I have not been disappointed by you! — That is a very beautiful folktale, child, but also a very sad one! I know the answer, but I don't know how I should make it comprehensible to you. Life will show you the answer first, unfortunately, show it unfortunately, and that will be very bitter for you. Two words I want to say to you, which both almost fit, one is 'poesy', the other is 'your own precious ego'. But do not think too much about it, ponder rather on new stories! And for now farewell, child! But I want to see you again! Come tomorrow towards midday to the lord's castle, and ask for the foreign professor. Will you come?"

"Yes!", little Jack said absent-mindedly. The stranger left. The boy searched mechanically for the whip, herded the cows together, and drove them onto the path. The two words which the stranger had spoken to him, and which were meant to be the answer to his folktale, sounded incessantly in his ear. But it was a strange, misunderstood sound.

Little Jack walked home very slowly, and when he raised his eyes, the evening sun blazed up in its golden brilliance, and went down straightaway. — —

"I beseech you, gracious lady, to believe me," the dark man said late in the morning of the following day to the lady of the manor; "it is really not the the physical beauty of the boy which won over the painter in me. I have had a look into this child's soul, and I was blinded, yes, was intoxicated by its noble beauty. In the image of this child's soul, there are no coarse lines, none of the usual, ordinary shading, there is light, struggling light which strives for brilliance and battles with ardent throes against the shadows which want to obscure it. My revered, gracious lady, help his light to victory!"

"Your enthusiasm honours both the artist and especially the man, Professor. I am also not averse to your idea of having the boy provided with a good education. But I would like to make two objections – firstly, the boy was strongly influenced by his mother, a Spaniard, and could have obtained his folktales from her; secondly, the people have nothing good to say about the boy himself."

"Concerning the first objection, my lady, it would not have occurred if you, most revered lady, had heard the boy's telling. Only a genius who has received a work from the muse herself and birthed it anew with his rendering has so much originality. And the second objection, it was your jest, you were smiling yourself when you were expressing it. If these village folk did *not* hate the boy, I would be enormously indifferent to him, for then the farmers would have to understand the boy, and he would be like them. No, my lady, anyone who has never been heavily attacked in their life, hated, impugned, scourged, gawped at by the stupid, and pitied by the mediocre, such a person is no genius!"

"What an advocate," the Baroness said, "the boy shall be accepted. Speak with him, Professor, he is your charge."

Now little Jack arrived. He was dressed as ever, calm as usual, and was not astonished even over the space which certainly seemed fairy-like in its furnishings.

"The stolidity of the strong," the Professor mumbled, then he said, "It is nice that you are so punctual, little Jack. This here is the Baroness."

"I know her," the boy said curtly. The Baroness screwed up her face a little, and behind the curtains someone drummed a few nervous taps on the panes.

"Can you not make compliments, little Jack?"

"No."

"Well then! You should tell the gracious Baroness something, little Jack!"

"She is not gracious!"

"Oh! But little Jack — why not then?"

"She told the mayor that father was a rough piece of work because he threw Bader."

The Baroness fanned herself agitatedly with her handkerchief, and behind the curtains a short, but very loud drumroll sounded. The Professor whispered to the Baroness, "Patience, dear lady," then he continued, "The Baroness did not hear the story told properly by the mayor; you tell it, little Jack!"

The boy was surprised by that; hence he cried out, "Eh, that can be done! That is good! The mayor, yes, yes, the mayor is an idiot who knows nothing but the story of the butcher Sepp. But I can tell the tale, that of father. Pay attention, Baroness!

Father loved mother and me a lot, probably mother most of all. He worked all day and kept no journeymen because he wanted to earn everything himself. From all the money which he received, he did not need much for himself. He ate a lot, but only cheap things. He did not go to the tavern, and he did not smoke cigars either. He did not ever swear. But he bought mother beautiful clothes and me beautiful toys. And for both of us, he bought books. He never read books, but he was happy if they delighted us. Grandmother sometimes grumbled. But then he just waved thus — with his hand thus, Baroness, and then grandmother had to be quiet. Do you see, Baroness, how father loved us?

When mother had died, and grandmother too, father had only me. He worked all day, but when I lay in the niche, he very often looked over to me. And when he was tired in the evening and I had to tell him a folktale

— one *must* tell folktales, Baroness — then he opened his eyes wide, even if he could barely keep his eyelids up — he was very good to me.

Then someone said something in the tavern about mother and me, something very nasty. He said we were mad. That was very stupid, but also very coarse. And then father wounded him — wounded — oh, if I had been there, I would have killed him, Baroness! For that father was locked away. In the fire station! I — I — thought that he would not survive being locked away, and I smashed in the fire station window, and brought him files. He should have flown, but he did not. Then I hated him. But now I know that it was good. Had we flown, I would have been happy and he miserable, and he should not be miserable."

"Child, child, come to me, and give me your hand. Your father is not a rough piece of work."

And little Jack offered the Baroness his tanned right hand.

"Poor child, you must have suffered a lot."

"I am not poor, and have not suffered much either. If something hurts me, I don't believe it or think of something else. That helps."

"What an imagination! — Now then are you a shepherd, little Jack?"

"Not a proper shepherd, for I don't look after the cows properly. But I am on the edge of the field when they are grazing."

"And what do you actually want to become, little Jack?"

"I don't know," the boy said sadly. "I must not stay with the farmers, I cannot be in the smithy either, and I cannot go away either. Previously I knew what I could become."

"Well?"

"An author, a great author! Mother once said it when I had invented a folktale, but I would have known it too if she had not said it. I know that I could become an author. I know a good many stories, and new ones occur to me daily. I can write too, though not as correctly as the schoolteacher wishes, but I can. If I were to become an author now, I would be able to write down everything I know, and all the people could read it."

"I want to assist you, little Jack, so that you can become an author."

Then little Jack gives a shout so that the man behind the curtain starts heftily.

The Baroness turns around to the latter, and says in French, "Please, Doctor!"

The tall gaunt man with the nervous facial expression and the glittering glasses steps out from behind the curtain.

"Baroness," he says obsequiously.

"Do a noble work in the service of humanity, Doctor, and teach this child next to my son."

"If you command it, Baroness!"

"I do not command, I request! Our Professor is right; in this child rests a treasure which must be raised. Be the digger for treasure, Doctor!"

The private tutor makes an irksome face.

"I hope that the Baroness is not disappointed by the boy."

"No, no disappointment, if you just help me, I will certainly become an author."

The Baroness turns around in shock.

"You speak French, little Jack?"

"Yes, I learnt from my mother! Mother travelled widely. She also spoke her native tongue, Spanish, with me, and sometimes English. She said I learnt Spanish very easily."

The Baroness looks at the Doctor.

Paul Keller

"I will attempt it," the latter says a little friendlier.

But the Professor calls out, "And when you have diligently learnt, little Jack, and have become great, then I will take you on a journey. There you shall see all the lands and then all the peoples —".

The painter cannot finish, like a wild cat the boy clambers up his tall figure, and — kisses him. — — — —

Christmas was long past. The frosts of January had covered the ponds with ice, the mists of February had brought much snow, and now the winds of March were blowing across the land and cleaning the air of all haze and chasing away all the hard frost.

Up in the castle, it made a terrible racket on the tall windows. Little Jack sat in the little room which had been put aside for him. Before him lay a Latin grammar and an exercise book for him to enter translations. But he was not writing, he had propped his head in both hands, and was listening to the wild melody of the storm.

Previously he would have been delighted by the glorious tune, he would have cheered along with it, and in his soul a fantastic little folktale would have occurred from the wild storm and its path and end. Now —

The door opens, and the Doctor enters. Little Jack, he who was usually never startled, starts.

"What startled you?", the private tutor said roughly, "only lazy students are startled by the teacher. Show me! Not — more? You have surely been dozing again or composing stories as you like to do? In your last work there were eleven crude errors! And then — of course! — rascal, are you unable to notice then that at the question 'Where to?', *to* is with the accusative? Write me as your punishment twenty sentences in which there is an accusative with *to*, understood?"

Little Jack nodded silently, and the private tutor walked up and down the room a few times.

164

# Forge Fire (A Character Study)

"Don't make such a pathetic face at me," he said, stopping again by the desk, "the Baroness might really believe how badly it goes with you. But I tell her that as long as you are under my charge, you must work, work hard, whether you may want to or not! Making things up and foolish talk has erected nothing in this world, only hard work has! Think of the splendid folktale about the forge fire. Had your father also always enjoyed the blazing up of the flames, childishly like you, then no iron would have ended up on the hoof and no rim on the wheel. No, the fire is there to serve, nothing more, and you are here to study, nothing more! Understood?"

Little Jack's demeanour does not twitch; perhaps he has not heard at all what the other person is saying. The latter gives the boy a not very friendly look and goes.

Little Jack does not stir from his place. The storm rattles monotonously on the windows, the boy stares motionlessly before himself; no letter enters the book.

What has become of little Jack! His face pale, almost wrinkled, and the eyes previously so beautiful now expressionless, weary! The boy seizes his head, it seems to him as if a heavy weight is loaded on his forehead, he feels for his heart which beats so lightly that he thinks it has died. How had all this happened?

He had thrown himself with a true zest at the studies, and yet the private tutor had managed to spoil it for him completely. What interested him passionately — history, geography, descriptions of nature — he was not permitted to pursue. The Doctor suggested that it nourished the disastrous, nasty imagination. Now little Jack sat by the grammar day after day. How easily he had comprehended the language teaching of his mother, how difficult did he learn a lesson when that man sat opposite him, who hated him and whom he did not love. The Doctor had an influence which had a paralysing effect on little Jack; nothing helped, nothing at all.

For a nature like little Jack's, there was no hindrance when it was permitted to make use of its weapon, of the strong, defiant power of the free soul. Had this power stood at little Jack's disposal, he would also have made the best progress in the old languages for which he was only mediocrely fitted. But the wings of his spirit were paralysed, paralysed by the hypnotic look of the false educator who, perhaps qualified to drive donkeys, did not have an idea of the psychology of inspired natures, and naturally could do nothing but disastrous, sinful errors of judgement.

The Baroness had also become cooler towards little Jack. The private tutor had understood to tell her that little Jack was of few gifts and not diligent, his spirit was wild, frustrated. Little Jack had noticed. Then all the old, harsh defiance of his soul was awoken anew, and he had wanted to raise a complaint against the tormenter of his soul and leave the castle. But then he had seen the eyes behind the cold glasses flash, he had fallen silent, and had remained. There is a power before which even the strongest soul of genius trembles, it is brutishness.

Little Jack steps to the window. The storm howls in terrible blows, and shakes a mighty oak. It bends its iron-hard branches, and now — splits them in two down the middle. Then the boy's eyes light up, "Hooray, you strong storm, now you have won, and send news of your triumph in a thousand sounds out to the trembling beings on the heath. How beautiful and strong you are, how cowardly and unhappy I am! Give me your defiance, give me my defiance back, or I must die!"

\*\*\*

Then came the salvation. It was on a rainy afternoon at the beginning of April. Little Jack again sat opposite his teacher, who was speaking in hard, disjointed sentences about the ablative absolute. Anyone who would have gazed into the boy's face and not paid attention to the dry stuff would have thought little Jack was spell-bound, enthused by the lecture. He was looking rigidly at his teacher, with brightly lit, sparkling eyes, and a fine redness covered his cheeks. The boy's being was so striking that even the Doctor noticed the change, but he daringly attributed it to his teaching.

Bitter disappointment! When the teacher began the rote repetition with little Jack, it appeared that the latter had not understood a syllable of any of it. The Doctor raged.

"Boy, rascal, did you listen at all?"

"No!"

"N—o? And you say that so casually? So — so — I — I — will knock you down, lout!"

All the furious man's veins are swelling, he raises his fist and plunges at little Jack. Then — he recoils! This boy has fire in his eyes, a green-black, terrible light flashes towards him, he sees two white fists ball and hears the words, dark, compelling, regal, "I cannot be struck!"

Then the furious man opens his fists, he stands there speechless, an image of disarmed brutishness. Then his eyes fill with hate, and he rushes out the door.

"Wait!"

The door crashes shut, the lock creaks, little Jack is locked in. The boy stands still for a while yet, then the spell is broken. A groan comes from his mouth.

"Miserable man! You want to be a teacher? You? You know that father comes home tomorrow, and must also know that my soul is all astir, and yet you want to force me to learn today, today! You are just as stupid as you are coarse!"

He looks at the table. There the books lie which that man had made him hate so, hated to death. A wild fury seized the boy, the window is opened with a jerk, and the books fly down into the garden. Then little Jack turns to the door. He finds it locked. That he had not previously heard of.

"Locked in! Me locked in? Me? Surely, you can lock in the cowardly boy to whom you gave bread and whom you mistreated during the lessons, that cowardly boy who lowered his eyes when he was unjustly rebuked, him, yes, quite certainly him, but not little Jack, not little Jack, hahaha, and I am little Jack again!"

With two strides, he is at the window. The room is on the first floor. The boy does not throw a look down. An exultant, echoing cry, "Free!", and he flies down. —

He remains lying unconscious for a little while. Then he gathers himself up. He feels pain, but he is able to walk; the ground on which he fell was soft. Next to him lie the books. Little Jack looks at them and ponders. Then a gleam passes over his face, he gathers the books up, and without once looking around to left or right, he hurries away from there.

Dusk has already broken; from the church tower, the last note of the evening's tolling dies away. Just then little Jack is walking past the open churchyard gate. He climbs up the few steps and walks between the graves. A little way away from the path lies his grandmother. Little Jack goes there. He sits on the mound, he places the books next to himself.

"Grandmother," he begins, "I come to you first, you know, I want to tell you something. You do not need to weed now anymore, and have good time to listen and pay attention.

I once told you a folktale, grandmother, do you still know the folktale of the forge fire? We were both far too stupid, you and I, to be able to understand it. Now I know what the folktale wanted to say, and I come to tell you it. It is a pity that you are closed up in the grave, you will not be able to hear it properly at all perhaps. But pay good attention!

I also told the folktale to the good Professor. You know nothing of him, but just believe that he is just as clever as good. He told me two words as a solution — 'poesy' and 'your own precious ego'. The first word only half fits, but the last fits totally. You will not understand it straightaway, grandmother, but it is not too difficult.

I have a soul, grandmother, which is precious, more precious than gold and as beautiful as the fire. Sometimes it merely glimmers in there, but when someone like the Professor comes, who speaks good, enthusing words, then they travel into the soul like the storm, and the soul blazes up like the fire, red, crimson, and hot and glowing, ah, and so beautiful, so beautiful! Then someone came with his teaching. He was like iron! Cold and brutal, grandmother, very cold and very brutal! But as he raised up the iron, my soul clambered up it. But he — he — when he had caught it — wanted to strike it dead, dead — much more, much more terribly dead, grandmother, than you are. But I, I thought that, when father struck the fire dead on the iron, it was sad, but not so bad because he can always ignite it anew, but if the Doctor struck my soul dead, it would never burn again. Hence I have run away. I must carry away my soul, he must never touch it again, never ever.

That is good, grandmother, isn't it? I had to tell you. But you cannot answer, and then it's very cold with you. That is why I will go again. Sleep well, grandmother, you must be very tired from all the weeding and working away in the smithy. What I also wanted to say was, tomorrow father comes, grandmother!"

The boy goes. He throws just a look at the grave of his mother.

"Not now," he says, "but I will come to you soon." —

The smithy lies in the dark of evening, dark, quiet, abandoned.

"The door is shut," little Jack said, but I can get in easily through the window by the garden."

He picks up a stone from the street and walks around the dark house. He throws the stone through the back window by the garden, then grabs through the shards and raises the window. Then he climbs in.

"Ah! Oh! Home!"

With shivers of delight, the boy breathes in the musty air, the air of his father's house. He stands motionless for a long time, giving in to the delight. Then he fumbles for a candle and lighter. He finds both. He places the candle on the anvil, and then he crawls into the niche. He straightens out and stretches his legs in cosy comfort.

"Home! Dear, dear niche!"

Then he squints across.

"Fire," he says, "fire!"

He searches for wood and spreads it out under the bellows. How it burns, he exults and tips coals over it. Now the coals are glimmering.

"Forge fire!", he cheers, "wait, I will bring you something which you will like to consume, and I will take pleasure in it."

He fetches the books. A rustling passes through the quiet smithy, the books are being torn up. And now the scraps lie in the coals and blaze up high.

"Hallelujah!" little Jack cries and, trembling with delight, covers his glowing face.

Then he tips coals on the fire again. He drags a chair over, grasps the handles of the bellows, and calls out, "Up, forge fire, up! Burn, blaze, shine, glow, gleam! Yes, gleam, gleam, gleam! It is a lie that the fire there is to serve, it is there to burn, to blaze, to gleam! Fire, you and my soul, we would both have to die if we were to serve. And now you shall not die, and now my soul shall not die, now no smith will come, and no doctor, now you both shall light up, gleam! You dear, beautiful, you hot, holy fire!"

The boy bends right over the glow. His face is unendingly beautiful in the red light, and his eyes sparkle, and the fire burns, and as if it wants to reciprocate the boy's love, it clambers onto the folds of his clothes.

Little Jack is in flames.

He grasps for his heart, the flames burn. —

There is a rattling at the door.

"Light in the smithy, open up!"

The flames burn.

A pane breaks, a man climbs in.

"Jesus! Child!"

The flames go out.

"Why — have — you — extinguished — them, — the fire — loved — me, — even if — it hurt — a lot. — The fire — knew — everything — everything — that would — come — later, — then it — was burning me — to death — because it's — so much better. — Mother — to — you —"

Little Jack is dead.

\*\*\*

The smith arrives the next day. He remains three days and three nights in the village. The he goes away. To where his sorrow carried him, nobody knows.

# About the Publisher

Our mission is to provide translations into English of the complete works of neglected major European writers. We do not cherry-pick works that seem the most marketable, but rather seek to provide a complete collection of each writer's works so that readers can follow the writer's development and decide on its merits for themselves.

http://www.facebook.com/KANitzPublishing

http://www.kanitzpublishing.com